A
CANDLELIGHT ECSTASY ROMANCE

the paperbackery
"previously enjoyed paperbacks"
1159 s. saratoga-s'vale rd.
san jose 446-BOOK
78 s. park victoria dr.
milpitas 263-READ

Candlelight Ecstasy Romances

1 THE TAWNY GOLD MAN, *Amii Lorin*
2 GENTLE PIRATE, *Jayne Castle*
3 THE PASSIONATE TOUCH, *Bonnie Drake*
4 THE SHADOWED REUNION, *Lillian Cheatham*
5 ONLY THE PRESENT, *Noelle Berry McCue*
6 LEAVES OF FIRE, FLAME OF LOVE, *Susan Chatfield*

THE GAME IS PLAYED

Amii Lorin

A CANDLELIGHT ECSTASY ROMANCE

Published by
Dell Publishing Co., Inc.
1 Dag Hammarskjold Plaza
New York, New York 10017

Copyright © 1981 by Amii Lorin

All rights reserved. No part of this book
may be reproduced or transmitted in any form
or by any means, electronic or mechanical, including
photocopying, recording or by any information storage
and retrieval system, without the written permission
of the Publisher, except where permitted by law.

Dell ® TM 681510, Dell Publishing Co., Inc.

ISBN: 0-440-12835-8

Printed in the United States of America

First printing—March 1981

THE GAME IS PLAYED

CHAPTER 1

"You can get dressed now, Mrs. Ortega, and I'll see you in my office in a few minutes." Helen smiled gently at the timid young woman with the dark expressive eyes, then turned and left the examining room.

Ten minutes later, after seeing the beaming girl out of her consulting office, Helen lit a cigarette and leaned back into her desk chair with a contented sigh. Maria Ortega's delight in having her maternal expectations confirmed had given her an all-over good feeling. Even after five years of private practice Helen still felt the same satisfaction on diagnosing a wanted pregnancy as she had the first time.

A buzz and blinking light on her desk phone brought Helen upright in her chair, hand reaching for the receiver.

"Yes, Alice?"

The no-nonsense voice of her R.N. Alice Kelly answered crisply. "Jolene Johnson is on the phone, Doctor. I think you'll want to speak to her yourself. I'll have her chart on your desk in a minute."

"Thank you, Alice." A long, slender forefinger touched the blinking button and in a tone professionally confident she asked, "What's the problem, Jolene?" Automatically glancing at the clock, Helen noted the time: one fifteen. Fifteen minutes into her half day.

Every Wednesday Alice scheduled patients no later than twelve thirty or twelve forty-five, depending on the medical requirements, in order to have the office clear of patients by one o'clock, thereby giving Helen one free afternoon a week. Helen hoped to one day achieve that free afternoon.

Now as she glanced at the clock she gave a small sigh. She had so wanted to get to that lecture at Temple this afternoon.

"I don't know if it is a problem, Dr. Cassidy." Jolene Johnson's young voice wavered unsurely. "But Tim insisted I call you."

Thoughts of free afternoons and lectures banished, Helen replied soothingly, "Suppose you tell me why your husband insisted you call me and we'll take it from there."

"Well, I have this odd little trickle. It's the strangest sensation. It started after lunch when I stood up to clear the table and it happened twice while I did the dishes. It's not like the book says happens when the water sac breaks, and I have no pain or anything, but it does feel funny."

As the girl was speaking Alice quietly entered the room and placed the open folder on Helen's desk. Helen nodded her thanks, lifted her oversize, dark-framed reading glasses from the desk, and slid them into place, her eyes scanning the neatly typed sheets for pertinent facts while a picture of Jolene Johnson rose in her mind. A pretty girl of average height and weight, she was twenty-three years old, married two years, and was one week into her ninth month of pregnancy.

"Your husband was right, Jolene." Helen's voice was calm, unhurried. "I want you to get yourself ready and go to the hospital."

"But, Doctor, I don't even have any pain!"

"I know, Jolene, but although you've had no gush of water, you are leaking and I want you in the hospital. I'll call so they'll be expecting you."

"Eh—I—" The beginning of fear in the young woman's voice was unmistakable. "Okay, if you say so." Then more softly. "Doctor, do you think something's wrong?"

"I doubt it, Jolene."

Helen's eyes had completed their perusal of the girl's chart and her voice was confident with the medical data she'd read. Jolene's pregnancy had been normal so far, with no indication of any irregularities. She'd have to examine the girl, of course, but she felt sure the girl and the baby were in no danger.

"Don't be alarmed. The hospital staff will take good care of you and I'll be in to see you later this afternoon."

Helen's quiet tone had the hoped-for calming effect, for the lessening of tension was evident in Jolene's voice.

"All right, Doctor, I'll do whatever you say, and thank you."

Helen sighed as she replaced the receiver and handed the chart to the silently waiting Alice.

"Trouble?" Alice asked quietly. The tall, rawboned woman had been a nurse for over twenty-five years. She had seen much, said little, and was impressed with very few. Helen Cassidy was one of those few.

"I hope not." Helen sighed again. Well, so much for free half days. "The girl's leaking but has no pain. Nothing very unusual so far, but we'll see."

Alice nodded briefly, then turned and left the room. Helen sat staring at the clock. If she left now, she'd be able to hear some of the lecture, but hearing part of a lecture wouldn't do her much good, so—she shrugged her slim shoulders resignedly—maybe next time.

In sudden decision Helen pushed her chair back, went to the closet, and removed her fur-trimmed storm coat.

January was being very unkind to the east coast this year, and the coat, along with the knee-high suede boots she wore, were not only fashionable, but necessary.

She slipped into the coat, dug in her capacious bag for her car keys, slung the bag's strap over her shoulder, and left the room, slowing her steps but not stopping as she passed Alice's desk.

"I'm going for lunch." She named a restaurant. "And then to the hospital, if you need me."

"Why don't you do yourself a favor and have a good meal for a change?" Alice chided dryly. "You're beginning to resemble your own shadow."

Helen heard the words as she closed the outer door. She was still smiling wryly as she unlocked the door to her Monte Carlo and slid behind the wheel. Alice had been on a fatten-up-the-boss campaign for several weeks now, and although her remarks were often pointedly barbed, they had failed to penetrate Helen's composure.

She was slender. She always had been slender. She probably always would be slender. End of story. Helen frowned. True she had been skipping some meals lately in order to keep up with her increasingly heavy schedule. Also true she had lost a few pounds, but at her age that was better than gaining weight.

An hour and a half later Helen walked into Jolene Johnson's hospital room and paused, a smile tugging at her lips. The head nurse stood by the bed, one hand outspread on the expectant mother's distended abdomen, her voice a dry, reassuring drawl.

"It's still in the attic. Relax, honey, it's going to be a long day."

As Helen moved quietly into the room the nurse turned and stepped back from the bed, a warm smile transforming her otherwise plain face.

"Hello, Doctor." Her tone matched her smile in warmth. "Jolene's doing just fine. All prepped and ready to go. At Mother Nature's convenience of course."

The Game Is Played

The tug at Helen's lips turned into a full smile. This brash young woman was the most flip, while at the same time, the most efficient nurse she had ever worked with.

"Thank you, Kathy."

The nurse nodded at Helen, sent a bracing grin at Jolene, and swung out of the room, whistling softly through her teeth.

Laughing, Helen placed her fingers on Jolene's wrist to take her pulse, eyes shifting to her watch. Jolene began speaking the moment Helen removed her fingers.

"Doctor, tell me the truth. Am I going to lose my baby?"

Helen paused in the process of adjusting her stethoscope, glancing at the girl sharply. "No, of course not. Whatever gave you that idea?"

"Well." Jolene's lips trembled. "I'm not due for almost a month and I have this horrible feeling that something's wrong."

"Just a moment," Helen murmured, then proceeded to give the young woman a quick, but thorough, examination. When she finished, she straightened and looked Jolene squarely in the eyes. "There is no indication that anything is 'wrong.' Now what I want you to do is relax. You may use the bathroom but I don't want you out of bed for any other purpose. I want you to rest."

"All right, Doctor," Jolene said softly. Then hesitantly, "May Tim come in?"

"Yes, for a little while," Helen replied, then added firmly, "but I want you to rest. The nurse will be taking your temperature and blood pressure hourly. Don't be alarmed, it's a precautionary measure. You are open to infection now and I want a periodic check just in case." She squeezed the girl's hand before adding, "Now relax and don't worry. I'll be back later to check your progress."

Helen walked out of the room, paused a few minutes

to speak to Kathy, informing her she'd be in the cafeteria if needed, then left the section.

As she walked along the halls toward the lunchroom, Helen smiled, nodded, and spoke to several of the doctors and nurses she passed, totally unaware of the admiring glances cast at her retreating back.

Looking tall and slender, her honey-gold hair drawn smoothly back from her classically beautiful face into a neat coil at the back of her head, Helen presented a picture of cool, calm professionalism. She lived up to that picture completely. It seemed she had always known she would become a doctor and had worked steadily toward that goal. During premed she had decided to specialize in gynecology and obstetrics and, except for a few minor and one major emotional entanglements, had concentrated all her energy in that direction.

Now, after five years of private practice and a flawless record, Helen had the reputation of being brilliant in her profession and coldly emotionless. She knew it, and she didn't care. In fact she encouraged the attitude. Even in the seventies achieving recognition in the professions was not easy for a woman. It took that little bit extra in dedication and hard work. Within her own sphere Helen had made it. If the cost was occasional weariness, due to a grueling workload, and periodic loneliness, due to her withdrawn attitude, Helen paid the bill and considered the price as minimal.

She had what she wanted. She led a well-ordered existence doing the work she loved. If, at rare intervals, the warm female inside yearned for male companionship, she squashed the yearning ruthlessly.

Helen was of the opinion that in any emotional encounter the odds were heavily stacked in the male's favor. She had been burned, badly, while still in her early twenties and had promised herself that never again would a man get the chance to hurt her. It had taken months for the emotional wounds to heal, and the scars still remained, a searing reminder of the arrogance of the male animal called man.

As she left the lunchroom, after having a soothing cup of tea, Helen heard her name paged. She went to the main desk in the lobby, lifted the phone, and gave her name. After a short pause Alice's voice came calm over the wire.

"Better put on your roller skates, Doctor, I think you are going to be a mite rushed. Mr. Darren just called. He's bringing his wife to the hospital now. Her contractions are four minutes apart. Good luck."

There was a small click as Alice hung up. Replacing her own receiver, Helen turned away from the desk with a silent groan. Why do they do it? she asked herself as she stepped into the elevator. Why do some of these young women wait at home until the last moment? Are they afraid and trying to put off the inevitable as long as possible? Or are they trying to prove how unafraid they are? Helen truly didn't know. What she did know was she could live without these last-minute rush jobs. And she had thought Kristeen Darren had more sense.

By the time Helen walked into the delivery room, properly capped, gowned, and shod, Kristeen was only minutes away from motherhood.

"Good afternoon, Kristeen." Helen's voice filtered coolly through the mask, which covered the lower half of her face. Above the mask her hazel eyes smiled warmly at the pale young woman. "Longing to have it over with and hold your baby in your arms?"

"Yes, Doctor," Kristeen began a smile that turned to a gasp as a hard contraction gripped her.

Helen's eyes shot a question at the anesthetist, who nodded and murmured, "Ready to go."

Less than twenty minutes later Helen walked out of the delivery room, leaving behind a very tired but ecstatically happy mother of a perfectly formed baby daughter.

After cleaning up, Helen went into Jolene Johnson's room, evicted young Tim Johnson with the assurance that he would be called when the time came, and spent the following twenty-five minutes examining Jolene and talking down her renewed anxieties.

"I want you to rest," she reiterated as she was leaving the room. "Sleep if possible. Conserve your strength for when your labor does begin. And don't worry, I'll be back later."

She was standing at the nurses' station, making notations on Jolene's chart and talking with Kathy when a nurse and a young student nurse rushed up to the desk all flustered and excited.

"You should have seen what we just bumped into, Kathy," the nurse, a dark-haired, attractive young woman in her midtwenties, said breathlessly.

Kathy eyed the two in amusement. "Good to look at, was he?" she asked dryly.

"Good!" The petite student gushed. "He was totally bad. Tall, red-haired, blue-eyed, and shoulders like a Pittsburgh Steelers linebacker. What a hunk," she finished in an awed tone.

Kathy, obviously unimpressed, shot a long suffering glance at Helen, who, lips twitching, opened her eyes innocently wide and fluttered naturally long, silky lashes at her, then turned and walked away without a word. Behind her she heard Kathy laugh softly, and the student nurse proclaim, "No kidding, Kath, he really was a hunk."

A smile still tugging the corners of her mouth, Helen pushed through the heavy swing doors that separated the labor and delivery rooms from the maternity section, thinking that, as Kristeen Darren was probably settled into a room by now, she may as well look in on her before leaving the floor.

The smile left her face on hearing her name mentioned as she approached the nurses' station.

"If Dr. Cassidy walked in now, we'd all catch hell." The

irate nurse, standing with her back to Helen, was so agitated, she missed the warning shake of the head from the gray-haired nurse she was speaking to. "But I can't budge them."

Before the older woman, who was facing both Helen and the angry nurse, could respond, Helen asked quietly, "What's the problem, Nancee?"

"Oh!" Nancee spun around, her face flushed with exasperation. "Doctor, it's the people in Mrs. Darren's room. There are five people in there, besides her husband. I've told them that, so soon after delivery, there should be no one in there *except* her husband, but they just ignored me. I understand that they're prominent people, and I didn't want to cause any trouble by calling security, but Mrs. Darren looks exhausted."

"There are six people around that bed?" The tone of Helen's voice sent a chill of apprehension down the spines of both nurses.

"I've tried to—" Nancee began.

"I'll go help her clear the room." The older nurse cut in.

"No, I'll do it," Helen stated grimly. "You two have more important things to do than trying to coax a group of unthinking people into behaving rationally."

Ignoring the anxious look the two women exchanged, Helen squared her shoulders and walked the short distance to the room in question. Pausing in the open doorway, Helen's eyes circled the room slowly, missing nothing.

Kristeen Darren did indeed look exhausted, even though her eyes were bright with excitement and pride. Her small pale hand was clasped tightly in a larger one, which obviously belonged to her husband, who, Helen noted with a frown, was sitting on the bed beside her. On either side of the bed were two older couples who Helen correctly identified as the respective grandparents. And at the foot of the bed was a young man, somewhere around thirty, Helen judged, who could be no one other than the "totally bad hunk," the giddy young student nurse had been starry-eyed over.

Helen's eyes lingered long seconds on the man. Up to a point the student's assessments had been correct. But only up to a point. He *was* tall and his shoulders did look like they belonged on a Pittsburgh Steelers linebacker. But this was no mere "hunk." This was more like bad news for all females. And his hair could not really be described as red. It was more of a deep chestnut-brown, the red highlights gleaming in the glare from the overhead light. And the face was shatteringly masculine. At least the profile, which was what Helen viewed, was.

"Is this party strictly family or may anyone join in?"

The caustic question, spoken in Helen's most professional, icy tone, jerked five startled faces toward her. Before anyone could protest or even open their mouths, Helen added, "As it seems to have slipped everyone's mind, might I remind you that this woman has just given birth, and although she did not have a very hard delivery, it is never easy. She is tired. She needs rest, and as I want to examine her, I will give you thirty seconds to vacate this room."

The startled expressions changed to embarrassment on all the faces but one. The "hunk" turned, giving Helen the full impact of rugged good looks, an ice-blue stare, and a voice loaded with cool, male confidence.

"You must forgive us, Doctor." The smooth, deep voice held not a hint of apology. "This is the first child born in both families for some twenty-odd years and I'm afraid we've all been slightly carried away with her advent." His eyes shifted briefly to Kristeen, clearly his sister, then swung back to Helen. "But I see you are right. Kristeen does look very tired." His eyes took on the glint of devilment. "If you would step out of the doorway, we will all file quietly out and leave you to do your job."

A shaft of hot anger stiffened Helen's already straight spine. This silken-mouthed young man was most assuredly overdue for his comeuppance. "Thank you," she snapped acidly, then turned away as if he were of no importance at all and addressed his brother-in-law in a pleasant tone.

"I'm sorry, Mr. Darren, but you really must leave now. If you have any questions about your wife's condition, please wait in the hall. I'll only be a few minutes."

As she was speaking she heard the muffled movements as the others left the room. When she finished, she favored the new father with her most disarming smile.

That young man grinned sheepishly as he grasped his wife's hand.

"No, Doctor, I'm sorry. We were all thoughtless and inconsiderate." He gazed down at his wife, his eyes warm with love. "I'm so proud of her, we all are, and yet we remained, tiring her even more. Our only excuse, as Marsh said, is that we got carried away. I have no questions, as you filled me in perfectly after the baby was born." He bent, kissed his wife lingeringly on the mouth, murmured a few love words to her, then straightened, released her hand, and stretched it out to Helen. "I'll get out of here now. Thank you, Doctor, for everything."

Clasping his hand, Helen laughed softly. "I didn't do anything. Kristeen did all the hard work."

The moment he was out of the room, Kristeen said quietly, "I must apologize for my brother, Dr. Cassidy. I know he made you angry, but you see, Marsh is used to issuing orders, not taking them."

"No matter." Helen brushed aside the subject of that young man. "Let's see how you've progressed." She did a routine check, asked a few questions, then, as she removed her stethoscope, pronounced, "Very good. Now, if you behave yourself, get some rest, and eat a good dinner, you may have visitors this evening." She started to move away from the bed, then paused and glanced archly over her shoulder. "Two at a time, please."

"Yes, Doctor." Kristeen promised meekly.

The hall was clear of Kristeen's visitors except for the "hunk" who leaned lazily against the wall next to the doorway, speculatively eyeing the passing nurses. As though he were invisible, Helen stepped by him briskly and headed down the hall. Silently, effortlessly, he fell into step beside her.

"I'd like a word with you, Doctor," the deep voice requested blandly.

Helen felt her hackles rise, followed by shocked surprise. What was it about this man that put her back up? For in all truth she had felt it the moment she'd clapped eyes on him.

"What about?" She bristled.

"Temper, temper," he murmured, then, at the flash of her eyes, "my sister, among other things."

Helen's steps didn't falter as she turned her head and raised her eyebrows at him in question.

"I've been told I was rude and owe you an apology by"—he raised his left hand and ticked off the fingers one by one with his right forefinger—"my mother, my father, my brother-in-law, and his most respected parents. By way of an apology let me buy you dinner."

Coming to a full stop in front of the doors into the labor and delivery section, Helen turned to face him, shaking her head. "No, thank you, Mr.—"

"Kirk, Marshall Kirk. Most people call me Marsh."

"I am not most people," Helen elucidated clearly. "Now if you will excuse me, I have a patient waiting." On the last word she pushed the door open, stepped through, and let it swing back in his face.

Jolene's condition was stable and unchanged. She had not had a twinge of pain, and as she was getting bored and restless with her confinement, Helen sat talking to her for some time. After briefly outlining the procedures she would take if Jolene did not go into labor within a reasonable length of time, Helen left the girl and stopped at the desk to speak to Kathy.

"Slow day," Kathy drawled, glancing at the clock. "And unless things start happening mighty quickly, I'll be off duty long before Jolene is wheeled into delivery."

Nodding in agreement, Helen's eyes followed Kathy's to the large wall clock, then flickered in surprise. It was almost six thirty! She had been in the section almost an hour and a half. No wonder she was beginning to feel slightly wilted and vaguely empty. Informing Kathy that she was off in search of sustenance, Helen left the section. The sight that met her eyes as she walked through the swing doors brought her to a shocked standstill. Propped against the wall, head back, eyes closed, stood Marshall Kirk, looking, strangely, neither uncomfortable nor out of place. On hearing the door swish closed, his eyes opened and appraised her with cool deliberation.

"Surely you haven't been here all this time, Mr. Kirk?" The frank admiration in that level blue stare put an edge on Helen's tongue.

"I assure you I have, Dr. Cassidy." The sardonic emphasis he placed on her name rattled Helen, giving an even sharper edge to her tone.

"But why?"

Sighing wearily, exaggeratedly, he closed his eyes. When he lifted the lids, he fixed her with an ice-blue gaze so intense that Helen felt a shiver curl up the back of her neck.

"I told you I wanted to talk to you about my sister. I also invited you to have dinner with me, by way of an apology."

Fighting the urge to rub the back of her neck, wondering at the odd catch in her throat, she rushed her words just a little. "That's not necessary, we can talk in the lounge right here or in the—"

"I know it's not necessary," he interrupted smoothly. "But it is now"—he glanced at the slim gold watch on his wrist—"close to seven. I assume you're hungry. I know I am. Why not have our discussion in a congenial atmosphere and feed the inner person as well?"

Helen stared at him wordlessly for a long second. What was it about this young man? She felt unnerved, a very rare sensation for her, and she didn't know why. Which, of course, unnerved her even more. His attitude, of polite interest, could not be faulted. Nor could his tone, for he sounded pleasantly reasonable. So what was it? Unable to find an answer, or a reason for refusing his invitation, Helen hedged.

"Mr. Kirk, I—"

"Yes, Dr. Cassidy?" He prodded gently.

"Very well," Helen sighed in defeat, then added firmly, "but I cannot go far or be gone too long. I have a patient in there"—she nodded at the large swing doors—"that I want to keep an eye on."

"Is she in labor?" he asked interestedly.

"Not yet." She shook her head. "But that's why I want to keep an eye on her."

"Whatever you say, Doctor." He paused, obviously thinking, then offered, "There's a small place, fairly close by, an old, renovated inn, would that do?"

"Yes, anywhere, as long as it's close by." Unsure she'd been wise in accepting him, Helen's tone was almost curt. "I'll need a few minutes. I must call my answering service, get my coat and bag and—"

"Take your time," he cut in. "I'll go get my car and wait for you at the main entrance."

Without waiting for a reply, he strode off down the corridor.

Her teeth nibbling at her lower lip, Helen watched him walk away, an uncomfortable feeling of foreboding stealing over her. She opened her mouth to call him back, tell him she'd changed her mind, then closed it again with a snap. *Don't be ridiculous,* she chided herself scathingly, there is nothing the least bit threatening about this man. He is exactly as he seems. A well-bred, urbane young man interested in the welfare of his sister. That his eyes seemed to have the power to demoralize her she put down to the fact that it had been a long day and that hunger was making her fanciful. Giving herself a mental shake, she walked away quickly.

He was waiting for her, standing beside a pale blue Lincoln Continental, hands thrust into the pockets of a perfectly cut tan cashmere topcoat. As her eyes ran over the luxurious garment Helen realized, with a start, that it was the first time she'd noticed his attire. If asked, she doubted if she could describe what he had on under the coat. Strange, she mused, hurrying toward the car, she usually took note of the total person, so to speak. Indeed, she could describe what Kristeen's parents, her husband, and his parents had been wearing, down to the snakeskin shoes the older Mrs. Darren wore on her small feet. Strange.

Preoccupied with her thoughts, Helen was only vaguely aware he'd helped her into the car and slid behind the wheel beside her, when his quiet voice brought her musings to an end.

"Problems?"

"What?" She blinked in confusion, then laughed softly. "No. No problems. I was just thinking."

One dark eyebrow went up questioningly and she was again subjected to that strangely intent blue gaze, then, with a small shrug and a murmured "Good," he turned away and set the car in motion.

A nervous, panicky feeling invaded her stomach and Helen turned her head to glance out of the side window, her teeth again punishing her lower lip. *What in the world*, she thought frantically, *is the matter with me?* She caught herself edging closer to the door and sat perfectly still with shock, her thoughts running wild. *Surely I'm not afraid of him?* Her hands went clammy as her stomach gave a small lurch. But that's preposterous, she told herself sternly. Over the last few years she had met, and had been unaffected by, a number of prominent and powerful men, some of whom had been extremely good-looking. What was it about this man? That she would react at all to him would have been curious. But this! This moist-palmed, all-over crawly sensation was mind bending. And to top it all off, he had to be at least five or six years her junior.

"You really are in a brown study." Once more that deep, quiet voice cut into her thoughts. "Wondering what your husband will say when he finds out you've had dinner with another man?"

It was a deliberate probe and she knew it. For some reason it irritated her.

"I'm not married, Mr. Kirk." Helen paused, then added bitingly, "As I suspect you already know, since I wear no rings."

To her surprise he laughed easily, slanting her a quick, glittering glance.

"No, Doctor, I didn't know, as a lack of rings today is no indication of a woman's marital status." All amusement was gone, replaced by mild disgust. "Quite a few of the young marrieds I know refuse to adorn their fingers with anything as possessive as a man's ring."

The knife-edged sarcasm to his tone shocked her and she stared at him in amazement. What in the world was he attacking her for? Did he think she was lying? The thought that he might brought her chin up in anger.

"I assure you, sir"—she bit heavily on the last word—"I have no so mistreated male hidden away."

"Temper, temper." He repeated his chiding admonition of a few hours earlier, then, "Ah, saved by our arrival at our destination."

The inn was old, but beautifully renovated. The decor was rustic, the lighting soft, and the fire that blazed in the huge stone fireplace infused the room with a warmth and welcome that went a long way in draining the anger from Helen.

THE GAME IS PLAYED

Sipping at a predinner glass of white wine, Helen studied him over the rim of the glass, taking deliberate note of his clothes. His brown herringbone sport coat and opened-necked cream-colored silk shirt looked casually elegant, as did the way he leaned back lazily in his chair, sipping his own wine. His eyes scanned the room disinterestedly, yet Helen had the feeling that not the smallest detail escaped their perusal. And for some unknown reason he scared the hell out of her.

"Will I pass muster, Doctor?"

Helen felt her cheeks grow warm at the amused taunt. She would have vowed he had not observed her study. Deciding attack was the best form of defense, she gave him a level stare.

"Does it matter, Mr. Kirk?" she asked dryly. "You are a very attractive young man, as I'm sure you know. I'm sorry if I was staring, but I can't believe you give a damn if you pass muster or not."

The sound of his soft laughter was more potent than the wine. The words that followed the laughter hit her like a blast of sobering cold air.

"Oh, but that's where you're wrong, Doctor. Your opinion of me is very important. For you see, my lady doctor, I fully intend to rectify the nudity of your left ring finger by encircling it with my wedding ring."

CHAPTER 2

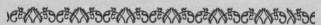

Stunned, speechless, thought and feeling momentarily turned off, Helen sat staring at him while the color slowly drained from her face.

Marsh stared back at her calmly, his cool blue eyes studying her reaction almost clinically.

She opened her mouth, then closed it again. How did one respond to a statement like that? If he'd issued it flippantly or teasingly, she'd have known exactly what to say, but he had been serious, deadly serious.

Feeling returned with anger that surged through her body and up under the delicate skin that covered her cheeks. Helen gritted her teeth against the hot, uncomfortable feeling.

"Mr. Kirk—" she began.

"Yes, ma'am?" Now he was teasing, the light of devilry casting a shimmery gleam on his eyes. Leaning across the table, he caught her hand in his, and when she tried to pull away, his grip tightened, almost painfully.

"If you call me 'Mr. Kirk' again, in that tone of voice, I swear I'll— The name's Marsh. Got that?"

Too angry to speak Helen nodded, glancing pointedly at

the large hand covering her own. When she glanced up, her eyes were as cold as her voice.

"Yes, I've got that, Marsh." Her voice lowered, but lost none of its brittleness. "Now if you don't remove your hand, I swear I'll stab you with my salad fork."

His soft laughter rippled across the table, surrounding her in a sudden, surprising warmth. His fingers tightened, somehow adding to the warmth, then he released her.

"Beautiful," he murmured. "My instincts were right. No wonder I fell in love the minute you started snapping at me in Kris's room."

Staring at him in astonishment, Helen froze in her chair, her eyes wide with disbelief at what she'd heard, disbelief and a touch of fear. Was this man some kind of nut? What had she let herself in for coming out with him? Glancing around the room like a cornered animal, Helen's eyes stopped on the waiter approaching the table with their dinner. Thoughts tumbled chaotically through her mind as she watched the waiter weave around the tables in the crowded room. Should she say she was feeling ill? Ask the waiter to call her a cab, while insisting Marsh stay and have his dinner?

"Relax, love." Marsh's soft tone cut gently into her thoughts. "And get that hunted look off your face. I'm not planning to abduct you or harm you in any way."

Helen's eyes swung from the waiter back to his and caught, held captive by the tenderness she found there. When the waiter stopped at the table, he sat back, his eyes refusing to release hers. The moment the waiter had finished serving and left the table, Marsh leaned toward her again.

"I promise I'll take you directly back to the hospital when we've finished." That blue gaze remained compellingly steady. "I also promise my pursuit will be ruthless." He smiled at the small gasp that Helen couldn't smother, then commanded gently, "Eat your dinner, you're beginning to look hollow eyed. There is all the time in the world to discuss this later. By the way—" he paused, frowned. "What the hell is your first name?"

The very abruptness of his tone brought an automatic response from her.

"Helen."

"Helen," he repeated softly, his eyes moving slowly over her face. She could feel the touch of those eyes, and a tiny shiver trickled down her spine.

"Yes," he finally murmured. "I like it. It suits you." He picked up his fork, held it suspended in midair. "By the way, Helen, I must warn you. My intentions are strictly honorable."

Helen was trembling. This conversation, this whole situation, was unreal. She had never seen him before this afternoon, yet there he sat, coolly telling her he intended to marry her. And those eyes! What was it about his eyes that set her pulses racing, caused this tight, breathless feeling in her chest? The room around her seemed to recede into a shrouded fog, the diners' voices grew dim and blurred. For a brief second out of time she was alone with him in that room. She did not know him, and yet it was as if she had known him forever. The mystical thought brought with it a dart of fear, followed by a shaft of excitement.

"Eat your meal before it gets cold, Helen." His tone was that of a concerned parent, coaxing a peckish child. It was exactly what was needed to break the spell of unreality surrounding her.

The room refocused, the voices took on human quality, and Helen began eating. Slowly, methodically, she made inroads into her food, tasting nothing. He watched her silently until she was almost finished.

"I didn't mean to frighten you, Helen. I only meant to make my position clear."

The very gentleness of his tone struck a nerve. Who the hell did he think he was? And did he think he was speaking to a toddling child? Or a doddering ancient?

The food in her stomach infused steel into her backbone and her head came up with a snap.

"You haven't frightened me in the least," she lied. "I've been around a few years, Marsh." She hesitated, then underlined. "A few more than you I think, and it will take a little more than a weird proposal of marriage to frighten me."

"Weird or not, I meant every word."

She had had enough. She was tired. It had been one very long day.

"If you don't mind, I'd like to go back to the hospital now."

"Of course." His sharp eyes contradicted his bland tone, and his following words gave her the eerie feeling he could read her mind. "You're tired and your day isn't in yet. Let's go."

As they made their way out of the room he placed a hand lightly at the small of her back. It was an impersonal touch, and yet Helen felt a tingle at the base of her spine that moved slowly, shiveringly up to her hairline. Annoyed, confused by her reaction to his slightest touch, she shrugged his hand away, quickening her step.

They were almost back to the hospital when she remembered the reason she'd gone with him in the first place.

"You said you wanted to talk about your sister." She glanced at his profile, sharply etched in the glare of the headlights from the oncoming traffic. A good profile: strong, determined, attractive. Trying to ignore her sudden lack of breath, she continued with a false calmness. "What is it about your sister's condition that bothers you?"

"Not a thing." The calm reply was directed at the street.

"But you said—"

"I lied." He shot a mocking glance at her. "I figured it was the only thing I could say that might get you to go with me, and I had to talk to you alone, tell you."

Helen felt that strange, disoriented feeling surrounding her again, and she shook her head violently to dispel it. "You don't even know me," she whispered hoarsely.

He stopped the car at the hospital's main entrance, then turned to face her.

"I will before too long." He lifted his hand from the steering wheel to cup her face, draw her to him. His thumb moved caressingly, disturbingly, back and forth across her cheekbone, then slowly to the corner of her mouth. "Don't look so shattered, love." His head moved closer, closer, and Helen couldn't tear her eyes away from his mouth. His lips a mere whisper away from hers, he murmured, "I don't understand it myself, darling. If I believed in reincarnation, I'd believe we have been lovers for a long, long time. I don't know. Hell, I don't even care. But I do know this. While I stood waiting for you in that hall, I knew I loved you and that you were mine."

Stunned, Helen's eyes widened as he spoke those incredible words, one thought screaming through her mind: *I've got to get out of this car.* His eyes held hers, motionless, breathless. His breath was warm against her face, the smell of the wine he'd had with dinner, mingled with the musky scent of his cologne, was intoxicating. When he finished speaking, she moistened parched lips, gave a strangled "No."

Too late. His mouth touched hers in a kiss so sweet, so tender, it was almost reverent in its gentleness. It destroyed her resistance and with a sigh she went limp inside the arms that were suddenly around her, hard and possessive. His lips left hers, moved searingly over her cheek, ruffled the hair at her temple.

"You're trembling," he said softly into her ear. "I know how you feel. I feel it too. Oh, God, Helen, I don't know what's happening. I've never felt like this before in my life."

Unsure, frightened, not at all the cool, self-contained

woman she knew herself to be, Helen stirred, tried to move away from him.

"I—I must go. I have a patient."

"No." His arms tightened. "Not yet."

His mouth sought hers again, but she twisted her head, began to struggle. The word "patient" had pierced the curtain of mistiness that had covered her mind, tore the veil of enchantment that had encircled her.

"Let me go, Marsh." Her voice was steady, controlled, the moment of madness had passed. "I want to go in . . . now."

Marsh sighed deeply but loosened his arms, then reached across her to open the door. "Okay, love, go to work." Dipping his head quickly, he gave her a fast, hard kiss. "I'll call you tomorrow."

"No, Marsh, I don't—"

A long finger came up to touch her lips, silencing her. "I'll call you tomorrow. Now go."

She went. Out of the car, up the steps, through the door, and across the lobby, practically at a run.

Waiting for the elevator, Helen glanced at her watch, then looked closer. Nine forty-five? That couldn't be the correct time! She swung around and her eyes flew to the large wall clock in the lobby. Nine forty-six. How could that be? The elevator doors slid back silently, and a frown marring her smooth brow, Helen stepped inside. She had been gone less than three hours, and yet it seemed such a long time since she'd left the hospital. Hours. Days. Half a lifetime.

A cold shudder shook her body as inside her head his voice whispered over and over again, "I don't know how. Hell, I don't even care. I knew I loved you and that you were mine."

The words jarred in her mind, tore at her nerves, like the needle caught on a badly scarred record. Nails digging into her palms, Helen stared, sightlessly, as the doors slid open at her floor. The doors whooshed softly as they came together and the car gave a mild lurch before it began to move up again. The lurch, mild as it had been, startled Helen back to awareness. Looking up at the floor indicator, she grimaced in self-disgust and stretched her hand out to touch the button of her floor number again. *What a fool you are,* she told herself bleakly. *You must need a vacation very badly.* The doors slid open once more and this time she stepped out quickly, walked down the hall with a determined pace.

Kathy was leaving Jolene's room as Helen crossed the floor toward it.

"Hang in there, Jo, you're doing fine." The nurse spoke over her shoulder, then turning, she flashed a smile at Helen. "That little lady means business, Doctor. She went into labor not long after you left and she's gone from one stage to the other like that." Raising her hand, she snapped her fingers three times in succession. "I just might have this baby before I go off duty, after all." She grinned.

Helen grinned back, a sense of normalcy returning with the easy flippancy of Kathy's tone. Marshall Kirk and the bizarre events of the last few hours were pushed to the back of her mind as Helen went into Jolene's room.

Several hours later Helen stood in another elevator, her fingers idly playing with the keys in her hand. Jolene's son, born less than an hour before, had weighed in at seven pounds two ounces, a lusty male, squalling his resentment of the whole procedure. Jolene was doing fine, sleepily content now that her fears were unrealized. A tender smile curved Helen's lips as she remembered the bubbling joy young Tim Johnson had displayed on hearing her news.

The car stopped at the sixth floor and Helen stepped out and walked slowly along the hall to her apartment at the front of the building, a sudden thought wiping the smile from her lips. Tim Johnson had seemed so very young to her, and yet he could not be more than a few years younger than Marshall Kirk!

THE GAME IS PLAYED

Hand none too steady, Helen unlocked her door, stepped inside, then leaned back against the smooth panels in sudden weariness. Memories of the few hours she'd spent with him flooded her mind, while a small shiver raced down her spine. What had possessed him to say what he had to her? Closing her eyes, she could almost hear his softly murmured words, feel his warm breath against her skin. Remembering the way she'd melted against him, her breath caught painfully in her throat. What had possessed her?

Opening her eyes, Helen pushed herself away from the door, hung her coat in the closet just inside the door, then walked unerringly through the dark living room to the small hallway that led to her bedroom. A flick of a switch cast a soft glow on the muted green and blue decor in the room, lent a sheen to the expensive dark wood furniture. Moving slowly, Helen sat down on the vanity bench, unzipped, then tugged the boots from her feet. Uncharacteristically she tossed the boots in the direction of her closet, then lifted her hands to remove the pins that held her hair in a neat coil. Freed, her honey-gold mane flowed rich and full to her shoulders, and Helen's fingers pushed through it to massage the scalp at the back of her head, gasping softly as the same tingling she'd experienced earlier that evening spread up her neck and under her fingers.

Stop it, she told herself harshly. *Stop thinking about him. He's a young man probably looking for a diversion, and an older woman is a challenge.* Her eyes shifted to the mirror, momentarily studying her reflection. The makeup she had carefully applied that morning, and touched up before going to dinner, had worn off, leaving exposed her clear skin, now pale and somewhat taut, with tiny lines of strain at the corners of her eyes and mouth.

It was a beautiful face and Helen knew it. She would be a fool not to know it and she had never been that. The honey fairness, the classic bone structure, the full soft mouth were gifts from her mother. Her height, her clear hazel eyes, and her determination were gifts from her father. Helen recognized and accepted those gifts with gratitude.

Now staring into those hazel eyes, Helen silently told her reflection, *he'll find no challenge here.* She had no intentions of getting involved with any men, let alone a younger one.

The mirrored eyes seemed to mock her knowingly. There was an attraction between them, she'd be a fool to deny that. The antagonism she'd felt on first sight should have warned her. Yet, she had never experienced anything like that before. How could she have known?

There was very little Helen didn't know about sex, except the actual participation in it. And that, she thought, biting her lip, was the most important part. What she had garnered from textbooks and lectures hardly qualified her as an expert. She knew what happened and the correct terms to define it, but without any real experience she was, in essence, abysmally ignorant.

Without conscious thought Helen brushed her hair and prepared for bed, her mind refusing to let go of the subject. She had come close, very close, to that real experience but she had backed away, almost at the last moment. And because of that long-ago fiasco she was still, unbelievable as it seemed, even to her sometimes, a virgin at thirty-five.

Slipping into bed, Helen lay still, eyes closed, wishing she'd not allowed her thoughts to stray in the direction they had. If she was still innocent, there had to be a reason, and her wandering thoughts had led to that reason. With a soft sigh of protest Helen saw a picture of a handsome, curly haired, laughing young man. Carl Engle, the man she had been engaged to while still in college.

Moving restlessly, she turned onto her side, trying to escape the memories crowding in on her.

She had been in love as only the very young can be, misty-eyed, seeing only perfection in the chosen one. They had seemed perfectly matched. They had shared the same interests in books, plays, music, movies, sports, and, most importantly, medicine. They had had wonderful times together; even studying had been fun, as long as they studied together. She had been seeing him exclusively for some months when he asked her to marry him and she had accepted him with only one condition: they would not marry until she received her M.D. Carl, who was planning on specializing in pediatrics, had agreed with a laughing "Of course. We'll make a great team. You'll deliver them and I'll take over from there."

Helen groaned and rolled onto her other side, her eyes tightly shut, as if trying to shut out the past. She was so tired, why did she have to think of Carl tonight? Marshall Kirk's face replaced Carl's in her mind and with another groan she gave up. Pushing the covers back, she left the bed, slipped into her robe, lit a cigarette, and walked to the large square window in the wall that ran parallel to her bed. Drawing deeply on her cigarette, she stared at the dark streets six floors below, lit, at this late hour, only occasionally by the headlights of a passing car. Glancing up, her eyes scanned the sky, following the blinking lights of a passing Jet Liner. The night was cold and clear, the stars very bright, seemingly very close. A shudder rippled through Helen's body and she drew jerkily on the cigarette. The stars had seemed very bright and close on that other night too.

She and Carl had been engaged six months and she was very happy, if vaguely discontent. Knowing what the discontent stemmed from was little consolation. Helen had been carefully brought up by loving, protective parents whose views on sex were rigid to the point of puritanical. She had been gently, but firmly, taught that a girl "saves herself" for her wedding night. The nights came, more often as the months went by, that Carl's love-

Amii Lorin

making became heated and his soft voice cajoled her coaxingly to give in. She had been tempted, filled with the longing to belong to him completely, to be part of him. But her parents had done their job well, and she had stopped him before reaching the no-turning point. In consequence she was left with mingled feelings of guilt and frustration. Guilt for having the perfectly normal urges that seared through her body, frustration at having to deny those urges.

That was the emotional situation on, what Helen had always thought of since, *that night*. They had driven over into Jersey to join friends at a beer and pizza bar to celebrate the end of first term. It had been a fun evening, with lots of laughter, as they solved the world's problems, decided who would win the up-coming Oscars, and discussed the merits of the latest rock groups. By the time the party broke up, Carl was mellow with beer and feeling very friendly. Instead of heading straight for the Ben Franklin Bridge to Philly he found a country road and parked the car off the side of the road under the trees.

Another shudder, stronger this time, shook Helen's slim frame and her arms came up to hug herself, her nails digging into the soft flesh of her upper arms. To this day every word, every act that had occurred in that car that night, was as clear in her mind as it had been then.

"Why are we stopping?" she had asked, glancing out the window apprehensively. The area was very dark and desolate, and the idea of being stranded there scared her. "Is there something wrong with the car?"

Laughing softly, Carl had turned to her, pulled her into his arms. "No, honey, there's nothing wrong with the car. I just couldn't wait to kiss you." His arms loosened, hands moving between them to undo the buttons on her coat. When the buttons were free he pushed the coat open, down, and off her shoulders, tugging it off.

"Carl!" she'd cried. "I'm cold."

The coat was tossed behind him as he slid from under the steering wheel, pushing her along the seat toward the door. "You won't be for long. I'm gonna keep you warm." His jacket followed hers, then his arms were around her again, jerking her against him with such force, it knocked the breath from her body.

"Carl, what—"

She got no further for his mouth crashed onto hers, jolting her head back with the impact. His lips were moist and urgent, his tongue an assault, and his hand, moving roughly over her back, slid between them to grasp painfully at her breast.

Shocked and angry at his rough handling, Helen had tried to twist away, her hand pushing at his shoulders. Her resistance seemed to inflame him and his arm slid around her again, crushed her against him. His lips slipped wetly from hers, slid slowly down the side of her neck.

"Come into the backseat with me."

His slurred words caused the first twinge of fear. It was not an invitation. It was an order.

"Carl, you know how I feel about that. I want—"

She gasped in shock and pain as his teeth ground together on the soft skin at the curve of her neck.

"Carl! Stop you're hurti— Oh!"

She hadn't seen his hand move, only felt the pain as his palm hit her cheek. His mouth caught hers again, grinding her lips against her teeth. Near panic, blinded by tears, Helen struggled, pushing against him frantically. Suddenly she was free as, pulling away from her, he slid back across the seat, cursing as he flung her coat and his jacket onto the floor, out of his way. He pushed his door open, then slammed it so hard behind him that the car rocked.

Sitting huddled and trembling on the seat, tears running down her face, Helen had thought he'd gone to cool off and she jumped when she heard him yank open the backseat door behind her. The door next to her was flung open, and with a grated "Get out," he reached in, grabbed her arm, and dragged her out of the car and around the backseat door. "Get in," he grated.

Nearly hysterical, Helen hit out at him, screaming, "No, I won't get in. I want you to take me home, now. I—"

"Damn you, get in."

This time it was his fist that hit her face, and barely conscious, Helen didn't even feel her shins scrape against the side of the car or her head strike the opposite armrest when he shoved her in and onto the seat. The next instant his body was on hers, pressing her back against the upholstery, one hand moving up under her sweater to clutch her breast, the other sliding up her leg under her skirt.

Her face, her whole head, throbbed with pain and she couldn't seem to focus her eyes. She felt groggy and sick to her stomach and still she fought him wildly, silently.

"It's your own fault, Helen. You and your damned wait-till-the-wedding-night bit. Well, I can't wait anymore, and I won't."

His mouth crushed hers and his larger body, pressing down on hers, subdued her struggles, cut off her air. Consciousness slipping away from her, Helen hadn't heard the car stop behind them, but she did hear the sharp rap against the window, did hear the not-unpleasant voice of the patrolman when he called, "Break it up, kids. You're not allowed to park here." Not waiting for a response, he strolled back to the patrol car.

Jerking away from her, Carl stared out the back window, cursing softly at the retreating, straight back. Then, turning, he looped his legs over the back of the front seat and pushed himself up and over. Glancing in the rearview mirror at the patrol car, obviously waiting for him to move, he cursed again, then snarled, "Well, are you coming up or not?"

Curled on the backseat, swallowing hard against the sobs that tore at her throat, Helen didn't bother to answer him. He waited a moment, cursed again, shrugged into his jacket, threw hers over the seat to her, then reached out to slam the door closed with a snapped "Will you shut the damned door?"

Moving slowly, Helen straightened and closed the back door. Then, pulling her coat around her shoulders, she rested her pounding head back against the seat and closed her eyes, gulping down the nausea rising from her churning stomach. They were almost back to her dormitory before Carl broke the strained silence.

"I'm sorry I hit you, Helen," he began softly, then his tone hardened. "But a man can take just so much. We're going to be married anyway, so what the hell difference does it make if we go to bed together now? No normal man could be expected to wait years to make love to his girl."

Again Helen didn't respond and she was ready when he stopped the car in front of her dorm. Without speaking, she pushed open the door, jumped out, threw his ring onto the front seat, and ran up the walk to the safety of the dorm, ignoring his call to wait.

Now, over ten years later, Helen stood staring out her bedroom window at a night very much like that other night, her face cold and uncompromising. Sighing deeply, she turned from the window, walked to the nightstand by the bed, shook another cigarette from the pack, and lit it, her eyes pensive.

Over the years she had gone out with many men, had proposals from several and a few propositions, but something inside seemed frozen and she could not respond to any of them. Intellectually she knew that all men did not become brutal when frustrated, but emotionally she could not handle a close relationship, and when a light good-night kiss began to deepen into something more or a male hand began to wander, she withdrew coldly, her manner shutting the man out as effectively as if she'd closed a door between them.

She had never been able to control her withdrawal, nor had she tried very hard to control it. In her opinion any woman who'd put herself in the position of receiving that kind of punishment twice was a fool.

Moving around the room restlessly, Helen tried to figure out what had happened to her built-in warning alarm that evening. Not only had she relaxed in Marshall Kirk's arms, she had, if only for a moment, returned his kiss. And the fluttering breathlessness that gripped her when he turned that steady blue gaze on her confounded her completely. *What the hell,* she derided herself, *got into you?* Strangely her mind shied away from delving too deeply for answers, and shaking her head sharply, she told herself to forget him. Which, of course, brought a picture of him to her mind.

Grimacing in self-derision, Helen dragged harshly on her cigarette, then crushed it out in the ashtray. Glancing at the clock, she groaned aloud. It was almost four and her alarm would ring at seven, she had to get some sleep.

As she slid between the sheets and drew the blanket around her shoulders, Marsh's murmured words taunted her mind. "I knew I loved you and that you were mine."

"Not on your young life, Kirk," she whispered aloud, then closed her eyes and drifted into sleep.

CHAPTER 3

"I don't know what it is, Doctor." Alice's voice was heavy with exasperation. "But I think everybody has a bad case of the Januaries."

Including me, Helen thought, a small smile tugging at her lips at the nurse's caustic tone.

"What now?" she sighed, cradling the phone against her shoulder as she lit a cigarette. It was her first one since lunchtime, and that had been over four hours ago. As usual for a Thursday the office had been full all day and that, plus her lack of sleep the night before, was beginning to tell on her. By the tone of her voice Helen suspected Alice was also beginning to feel a little hassled.

"There is a patient in the other examining room, there are four more still in the waiting room, and I have a Mr. Kirk on the line who insists on speaking to you. I've told him you are very busy, but—"

"It's all right," she cut in wearily. "I'll talk to him."

There was a short, somewhat shocked, pause and then a click.

"What can I do for you Mr. Kirk?" she asked coolly.

Soft laughter skimmed through the wire to tickle her ear.

"Do you want the proper answer or the truth?"

"I'm keeping a patient waiting." Helen's tone plunged five degrees.

"Where have I heard that before?" he wondered aloud, then, "okay, I'll be brief. What time should I pick you up for dinner, and where?"

Caught off guard by his casual assumption that she'd go with him, Helen searched for words. "Mr. Kirk," she began after several long seconds.

"Yes, darling?" It was a smooth warning Helen couldn't ignore.

"Marsh." She bit the name out through clenched teeth.

"That's better," he crooned.

"Marsh," she repeated coldly. "I do not have time to play telephone games. I had very little sleep last night and a very busy day today *and* I won't be through here for another hour and a half. I am tired and I don't feel like going out to dinner."

"Okay," he replied easily. "Come right to my place when you leave the office and we'll eat in."

This man had a positive talent for striking her speechless.

"I certainly will not come to your place," she finally snapped.

"I'm inviting you for dinner, Helen." The amusement in his voice made her feel very young and naive. "Not for a long, illicit weekend."

"I don't—"

"Good Lord, Helen," he cut in briskly, all amusement gone. "You're not afraid of me, are you?"

"No, of course not, but—"

"No, of course not," Marsh mimicked. "I'll expect you in about two hours." He rattled off an address, then his tone went low with warning. "And if you're more than fifteen minutes late, I'll come looking for you."

The line went dead before she could answer him, and Helen stared at the receiver, anger, mixed with a flutter in her stomach she refused to acknowledge, bringing a twinge of pink to her pale cheeks. Of all the arrogant gall, she fumed. Just who in the hell did he think he was anyway? Well, he could go whistle up his hallway. She had no intention of going to his place for dinner, or anything else.

The following hour and fifteen minutes seemed to fly by and Helen caught herself glancing at her watch more and more frequently. By the time she ushered her last patient out of her office, Helen was having a hard time hiding her nervousness. Would he really carry out his threat to come looking for her? Of course he wouldn't, she told herself bracingly. Of course he would, her self chided positively.

Undecided, Helen fidgeted, moving things around on her desk aimlessly. Alice came to the door to say good night, a puzzled expression on her face at Helen's unusual behavior. Her mind playing a tug of war with "to go or not to go," Helen didn't notice Alice's concerned look.

The second hand on her desk clock seemed to be sweeping the minutes away in less than thirty seconds each. Finally, with barely enough time left to reach his apartment within the time limit he'd set, Helen dashed into the changing room that connected her two examining rooms. Fingers trembling, she smoothed her hair, tucked a few loose tendrils into the neat coil, then did a quick repair job on her makeup.

Tension kept Helen's fingers curled tightly around the steering wheel as she inched her way through the early evening traffic, her eyes darting to her watch at every stop sign and red light. The address Marsh had given her was a large, fairly new condominium just outside the city limits, with a spacious parking area off to one side.

A security guard sat at a counterlike desk just inside the wide glass entrance doors, and the first thing Helen noticed was the clock that sat on the desktop next to a registration book. She was two minutes inside his time limit. She gave her name and the security guard said politely, "Oh, yes, Dr. Cassidy, Mr. Kirk called down that he was expecting you. You may go right up. Apartment eight-oh-two to the left of the elevator."

He indicated the elevator across the foyer behind him, then bent to write something in the register. *Probably my name and the time of arrival*, Helen mused as she crossed the dark red-carpeted floor.

A few seconds later, standing before the door marked 802, Helen drew a deep breath, held it, and touched her finger to the lighted doorbell button. The door was opened almost immediately, convincing her that the guard had announced her arrival, and once again she was held motionless in a hypnotic blue gaze.

"Perfect timing," Marsh murmured, pulling the door wide as he stepped back. "I had just decided to give you a few more minutes before going on the hunt." His mouth curving into a smile, he taunted, "Are you coming in or are you going to bolt for the exit?"

Giving a good imitation of a careless shrug, Helen exhaled slowly, broke the hold of his eyes, and stepped inside. Every nerve in her body seemed to jump when the door clicked shut behind her and hum like live electrical wires when she felt his hands on her shoulders.

"I'll take your coat."

His soft voice, close to her ear, turned a mundane statement into a caress, and Helen bit down hard on her lip to try and still the shakiness of her fingers fumbling at her coat buttons.

When he turned away to hang up her coat, Helen's eyes swept the oversize living room, glimpsed the dining room behind an intricately worked wrought-iron room divider. The colors in the room merged and blurred before her eyes as she was spun around and into his arms.

"I thought you'd never get here."

Marsh's eyes had a dark, smoldering look and his voice was a rasp from deep in his throat.

Helen's arms came up between them, her hands pushing ineffectively against his shoulders.

"Marsh—"

His head swooped low and his mouth caught her parted lips, silencing her protests. His lips were hard with the demand for her submission, his kiss possessive, consuming.

Feeling reason beginning to slip away, Helen's mind sent an order to her hands to pull his head away. Her hands lifted, her fingers slid into his hair, but somewhere along the line the order became garbled and instead of tugging at his hair, her hands grasped his head, drawing him closer. At once his arms tightened, molded her against the long, taut length of his body. His mouth searched hers hungrily, making her senses swim crazily and igniting a spark that quickly leaped into a searing flame that danced wildly from her lips to her toes. Teetering on the edge of surrender, Helen murmured a soft protest when his mouth left hers. Leaving a trail of fire, his lips moved slowly over her cheek. His teeth, nibbling at her lobe, sent a shaft of alarm through her, and reason scuttled back where it belonged. Her hands dropped onto his shoulders and pushed, using all the strength she possessed.

"Marsh, stop, I've got to call my service."

"Later," he growled against the side of her neck. "Helen, I've waited all last night and all day today to hold you like this. You can call your service later."

His lips found, caressed, the hollow at the base of her throat, and Helen, her breathing growing shallow and uneven, knew that if she didn't put some distance between them her will would turn to water. She pleaded, "Marsh, please. I must let them know where I can be reached. Let me go, please."

For a long moment she thought he was going to disregard her plea, then, with a low moan, his arms dropped and he stepped back, a rueful smile curving his mouth.

"Be my guest."

He waved his hand negligently at the living room, and turning, Helen's eyes sought, then found, the phone resting on an octagonal-shaped cabinet table at the end of a long sofa, which was covered in a gold furry material.

On legs she was none too sure would support her, Helen made her way to the phone, stumbling a little when she caught her boot heel in the deep plush of the chocolate-brown carpet.

"Careful, love."

The softly spoken caution threatened to sap the remaining strength from her legs, and Helen sank onto the corner of the sofa with a soft sigh of relief. As she punched out the services number on the push buttons, she heard Marsh walk across the room and glanced up to see him disappear into the dining room.

"Come into the dining room."

His call, obviously from the kitchen, came as she replaced the receiver, and drawing a steadying breath, Helen rose and walked into the room just as he emerged from an opposite door.

"I hope you like Chinese food." He grinned easily. "I stopped and picked it up on my way home."

He held a long-stemmed glass, three quarters full of white wine, in each hand and he moved with such casual ease, Helen felt a hot flash of anger. What had happened to all the tension that had tautened his entire body only a few minutes ago? She felt on the point of collapse, while he looked relaxed and unaffected. Could he flick his emotions on and off like a light switch?

"Are you going to take the wine?" His chiding tone made her aware of the glass he was holding out to her. "Or are you going to scowl at it all night?"

Embarrassed now, not only by her present vagueness but by her response and subsequent reaction to his advance, she lifted her eyes and stared into his with a steadiness she was far from feeling.

"Is white the correct wine for Chinese food?" Her attempt at lightness didn't fall too short of the mark.

"Who cares?" His shoulders lifted eloquently. "I drink what I like with whatever I choose to eat." His eyes glittered as he placed the glass into her hand. "I please myself and never worry about what others deem correct."

Positive his last remark held a double meaning, also positive she would not be able to eat a thing, Helen allowed Marsh to seat her at the table. When he went back into the kitchen for the food, she sipped tentatively at her wine, identified it as an excellent Chenin Blanc, then drank some more in an effort to relax the tightness in her throat.

Marsh hadn't forgotten a thing. He began talking the minute they'd started on their wonton soup and kept up a steady flow of light conversation right through the chicken chow mein, fried rice, and shrimp egg rolls. By the time she bit into her almond cookie, Helen had not only relaxed, she found herself laughing delightedly as he recounted the Christmas Day antics of a friend's youngster.

"Give me a minute to clear the table and stack the dishwasher, then we can have our coffee in the living room," Marsh said when the last cookie crumb had disappeared. "Or would you prefer more wine?"

"No, thank you." Helen shook her head emphatically. "I've had more than enough. But I would love some coffee and I'll help you with the cleaning up."

They made fast work of the table and dishes, then Helen preceded him into the living room, sat on the sofa, and watched as he placed a tray with the coffee things on the low coffee table in front of him, then turned and walked to the stereo unit along the wall next to the dining room entrance. He selected a long-playing record from a large, solidly packed record cabinet, put it on the machine, then came back to her and, to her amazement, instead of seating himself in the opposite chair or on the sofa beside her, he dropped onto the floor, stretched his long legs out, and rested his back against the cushion, next to her legs.

The opening strains of Tchaikovsky's *Romeo and Juliet* filled the room as she poured the coffee, handed him his, then sat back, her eyes following the direction of his to the flickering coils of a conal-shaped electric fireplace set in the wall between two large drapery-covered windows.

They sat in listening silence, both of them held in quiet captivity to the composer's genius. Even when Marsh held up his cup for a refill, she filled the cup and added more to her own without either uttering a murmur. When he finished his coffee, he placed the cup on the tray, shifted his shoulders, and rested his head against her thigh.

Replete with food, heavy lidded from lack of sleep the night before, Helen let her head drop back against the sofa and closed her eyes, the hauntingly beautiful music moving through her body like a living thing. Unaware of her actions, her hand dropped idly to his head, slim fingers slid slowly through the silken strands of his hair.

Trembling, her emotions almost painfully in tune with the music's throbbing finale, it seemed the most natural thing in the world when his fingers circled her wrist, drew her hand across his face to his mouth. His lips, moving sensuously on her palm, sent a spreading warmth up her arm, increasing the trembling, robbing her of breath.

"Marsh."

Her soft involuntary gasp set him in motion. Grasping her wrist, he levered himself up and onto the sofa beside her, drawing her arm around his neck as his head moved toward hers. His free hand caught her chin, tilted her head back, ready for his mouth. His kiss was the exact opposite of the night before. His lips, hard and demanding, forced hers apart, took arrogant possession of her mouth with driving urgency. His hands moved between them to expertly dispatch the buttons of her shirt. A sensation strangely like déjà vu flashed through her. It was gone in a moment, replaced by the new, exciting sensations his hands, sliding around her waist, sent shivering through her body.

Holding her firmly, he turned her, lowered her slowly to the soft cushions, and without knowing quite how he'd managed it, she felt his long length stretched out partly beside, partly on top of her.

His mouth released hers, went to the hollow at the base of her throat, his lips, the tip of his tongue, teasing a soft moan from her constricted throat.

"Marsh, you must stop. I'm so sleepy. I have to go home, get to bed. Oh, Marsh—"

His lips had moved down, in a fiery straight line, to explore the shadowed hollow between her breasts.

"You don't have to go anywhere." His warm breath tingled tantalizingly over her skin as his mouth moved back to hover over hers. "Your service knows where to reach you. If you're that sleepy, you can sleep here, with me."

"No, I—" His lips touched hers lightly, fleetingly. "I can't stay here." Her lower lip was caught between his. "It's—it's out of the question." His teeth nibbled gently at the sensitive inner ridge of her lip. Her voice sank to a low cry. "Oh, Marsh, kiss me."

His mouth crushed hers, causing a shudder to ripple along the length of her body. The flick of his tongue against her teeth drove her hands to his chest, trembling fingers fighting his shirt buttons. When her palms slid over his hair-roughened skin, he lifted his head, groaned, "Stay with me, Helen. Sleep with me. Let me show you what you do to me."

"I can't—I—what are you doing?"

He was on his feet, lifting her in his arms. Turning, he carried her across the room, through a doorway. "You said you wanted to go to bed." He kicked the door closed, walked to the bed, then stood her on her feet in front of him.

"Not here!" Her hands were drawn back to his chest as if magnetized. "Marsh, I can't stay here. Stop that!"

Disregarding her order, his fingers continued to tug the pins from her hair. When her hair was free of its confining coil, his hands dropped to her shoulders. With a minimum of effort her shirt was removed, dropped carelessly onto the floor. "Marsh, don't," she pleaded softly. "I want to go home."

Again that odd flash of déjà vu struck her. In confusion she wondered what had caused it, then her thoughts became blurred as Marsh's lips found a sensitive spot behind her ear.

"You're so beautiful, Helen." Her legs went weak at his low tone, the enticing movement of his lips on her skin. "Stay with me." His hands slid smoothly over her back. His fingers flipped open her bra with easy expertise. The lacy wisp of material landed on top of her shirt. "I want you so desperately." His hands slid around her rib cage.

"Marsh, no!"

His mouth silenced her weak protest at the same moment as his hands moved up and over the full mounds of her aching breasts. Reason fled and with a soft sigh she wound her arms around his neck, clinging as he slowly lowered her onto the bed. His mouth devoured hers, his tongue teased hers. Her skirt was twisted around her hips, and one hand deserted a hard-tipped mound to caress her nylon-clad thigh.

Moaning softly, barely aware of what she was doing, her hands came up to clasp his head, fingers digging into his hair ruthlessly to pull him closer, wanting more and more of his mouth.

She heard him groan before he moved over her, his solid weight pushing her into the firm mattress. Suddenly she froze. The feeling of déjà vu gripped her and she was being pressed against a cold car seat. Carl's face rose before her, filling her mind with fear. Tearing at his hair, she forced his mouth from hers with a hoarse cry.

"Damn you, stop it."

Marsh jerked away from her as if he'd been shot.

"Helen, what is it? Did I hurt you?"

Shaking with remembered panic, she didn't hear the words. All that registered was that the voice was male, and it terrified her. Cringing away from him, she brought her forearm up across her face, fingers spread to ward off a blow. The voice that whispered through her lips belonged to a younger woman.

"Don't hit me again, please."

Marsh froze, staring at her in disbelief.

"Hit you? Helen, what the hell—"

"Carl, please don't." She was sobbing now. "Please."

At the sound of the other man's name Marsh's face went rigid, lids narrowing over eyes ice-blue with fury.

"He hit you?" He gritted. "This . . . Carl . . . he dared to hit you?" His tone went low with menace. "If I ever find him, I'll kill him."

His cold tone, the words that were not a boast or even a threat, but a statement in the absolute, broke the hold of memory gripping Helen's mind. The back of her hand slid down to cover her mouth.

"Oh, God, Marsh." Her eyes went wide to stare into his. "It was so real, so horribly real. It was all happening again."

Sitting up fully, he grasped her shoulders, pulled her up, over his legs. Cradling her in his arms like a child, he asked, "When did it happen?"

Closing her eyes, she sighed wearily, "Long ago. So very long ago, and yet it seemed so real just now, as if it were all happening again." A shudder tore through her body, and his arms tightened protectively. She buried her face in the wiry mat of curls on his chest, her wet tears making a few strands glisten.

"He raped you?"

The words came softly from his lips, but Helen heard the tone that spoke of tightly controlled rage.

"No. No." She shook her head, her forehead rubbing against his chest.

"A—a patrol car stopped. The patrolman told him he'd have to move along."

Helen felt the shiver that slithered through his tough body, heard the sigh that escaped his lips. His arms tightened still more.

"You called to the cop for help?"

"No." Silent tears slid down her cheeks. "You don't understand, Marsh, I was engaged to him." She shivered. "I thought I wanted to spend the rest of my life with him."

"Don't cry, love." His fingers brushed at her wet cheeks, smoothed the hair back from her temples. "You've been afraid ever since?"

"I guess so." She gave a small shrug.

"This has happened before, when you've been with other men?" He paused, then added stiffly, "Or is it me that repels you?"

"It has never happened before because I've never been with any other men. I don't know—"

"What?"

He went completely still. After several seconds Helen lifted her head to see his face. The face he turned to her was one of total astonishment.

"You have never been—?" He broke off, his voice mirroring his expression. "Helen, are you still a—"

"Yes." Helen rushed before he could say the word. "Yes, yes. There has never been anyone."

"Well, I will be damned." He murmured softly. "I've changed my mind." He bent his head, kissed her lightly, a small smile tugging at his lips. "I'm not going to kill him. I'm going to thank him for saving you for me."

"He didn't save me for you or anyone else," Helen snapped. "I lost my head tonight but it won't happen again."

His hand caught her face, drew it close to his.

"Not for a little while, maybe. I'm going to give you time to get to know me. I'm going to get to know you. But it will happen again. Nothing can stop it. I told you you are mine. Nothing you do can change it. A little while ago, before the memories caught you, you were mine. We're going to be fantastic together."

He released her abruptly and stood up. "But not tonight. Right now I'm going to get the hell out of here so you can get dressed. Then I'm going to take you home." Bending swiftly, he kissed the tip of each full breast, then brought his lips to her mouth. "You have a beautiful body," he whispered between short, hard kisses. "I love it and I love you. You may not be ready to face it yet, but you love me too."

Laughing softly at her outraged gasp, he strode across the room, bathing the room in light by the flick of a switch as he went through the doorway.

The moment the door closed, Helen jumped off the bed. She was wide awake, all her earlier sleepiness banished by the events of the last hour. Moving slowly, she tried to explain away the strange experience, make some logic of it in her own mind. What she'd told Marsh was true; nothing like it had ever happened to her before. She'd had frightening nightmares for some months after the incident, but they had eventually faded. During the last few years she'd rarely thought about it, and when she did, the memory was triggered by odd, unrelated incidents. Even meeting Carl, which she did occasionally, had not disturbed her. Except, her reasoning qualified, that very first time, and she had come away from that meeting with her head high, her poise and cool composure intact.

Helen used the bathroom that was off his bedroom, absently admiring the masculine-looking marbled black and white tile, the large snow-white bathsheets. The long glass shelf under the medicine cabinet held just three items: his shaving cream, his aftershave, and the cologne that, on his skin, had the power to make her senses swim.

Fully aware of her surroundings now, Helen went back into the bedroom, her eyes making a cool survey. The bed, which she'd only seen in semidarkness before, was kingsize and, right now, very rumpled. Like the bathroom, Marsh's bedroom reflected the man. Totally masculine, with an understated core of warmth.

Agitated at herself for her softened attitude toward him, Helen tossed back her hair impatiently. Within minutes she slipped into her bra and shirt, then on hands and knees she retrieved most of the hairpins he'd dropped carelessly to the floor.

Rising to her feet, she raked her fingers through her tangled hair. Wincing at the twinge of pain on her scalp, she walked to the door, pulled it open and called irritably, "Marsh, will you hand me my handbag, please? I need my hairbrush."

Tapping her foot impatiently, Helen watched him scoop her bag off the floor beside the sofa, then saunter to her, a smile curving his lips at her disgruntled expression. His eyes slid over her slowly, thoroughly, before coming back to study her face, her hair.

"I don't know why you want your brush," he teased, his eyes glinting with devilry. "You look ravishing with your hair all wild around your face." He paused, head tilted to the side, considering before adding softly, "Or is the correct word 'ravished'?"

Giving him a sour look, Helen snatched the bag from his hand, rummaged in it for the brush, then, tossing the bag onto the bed, she turned her back to him and walked to stand in front of the large mirror above the double dresser.

THE GAME IS PLAYED

His reflection told her that his eyes followed her every move and, made nervous by his perusal, she pulled the brush through her knotted mane with unnecessary force. Tears sprang to her eyes from the self-inflicted pain. Pausing in midstroke, she blinked her lids rapidly to clear her vision and thus missed the reflection beside her own growing larger. The sound of his voice close behind her made her jump.

"What are you punishing yourself for, love?" His fingers plucked the brush from her hand. "Nothing happened here tonight that shouldn't have happened long ago." Very slowly, very gently, he drew the brush through her hair. "Don't misunderstand. I am, egotistically, very happy that it did not. You are mine and the thought that you have belonged, however briefly, to another—or several other—men has been tearing my guts apart since I left you at the hospital last night."

The brush was tossed onto the dresser, and with a shiver she felt his hand draw aside her now-smooth and shining mane, felt his lips caress the sensitive skin on the back of her neck. The shiver increasing in intensity, she heard him draw deeply the scent of her into his lungs, felt the delicious tingle of his breath as he exhaled slowly.

"I'm nearly out of my mind with love for you, Helen. And I want you so badly, I can taste it. But I can wait until my lovemaking doesn't activate the ugly memories. Until I hear, from your own lips, that you want me every bit as badly as I want you. But, dear God, love, I hope the waiting period is a short one."

As he spoke he turned her around, into his arms, his intense blue gaze staring into her wide, wary eyes.

"Marsh," she began firmly enough. "I wish you wouldn't talk like this. I don't want to get invol—"

His mouth covered hers, effectively cutting off what she'd been about to say. Undaunted, Helen began speaking again the instant he lifted his head.

55

"Marsh, listen to me. I don't want any kind of emotional involvement. Besides which——" she hesitated, wet her dry lips, then said flatly, "I'm older than you."

A deep frown brought his dark, beautifully shaped eyebrows together. A tiny fire leaped in his eyes.

"Did you think I was unaware of that?" Just the sound of his quiet voice made her shiver. "Exactly how old are you?"

Helen's eyelids lowered, then came up again defensively. Never before had she hesitated about stating her age. The fact that this man could make her feel defensive about, resentful of, her years was a shocking bit of self-knowledge she didn't want to face. In retaliation she forced a note of pride into her voice.

"Thirty-five."

"And I'll be thirty-one in March." His shrug was eloquent. "I hardly think four years is just cause for argument."

His blithe unconcern angered her. Jerking her shoulder away from his hand, she turned away.

"Four years can be very important."

She was immediately swung back to face him. His hand grasped her chin, held it firmly.

"The only years that hold any importance for me any longer are the years we are going to spend together."

At her wince the pressure on her chin was eased, although he did not let her go.

"I'm not going to argue about this anymore tonight, Helen." He lowered his head and Helen's eyes became fascinated with his mouth. "I knew from the moment I laid eyes on you that we belonged together. Nothing you say, nothing you do, is ever going to change that."

His lips were almost touching hers and Helen tried to ignore and deny the warm curl of anticipation in her stomach.

"There isn't anywhere on this earth you could run to

to get away from me, or yourself for that matter. Now close your eyes like a good girl, because I'm going to kiss you."

And suiting action to words, he did, his arms sliding around her to draw her close against him. The kiss was long and deep and wildly arousing, and Helen could no more have stopped her arms from clinging to him, any more than she could stop the passage of time. She felt a tremor run through his body before he put her firmly from him. Eyes smoldering with smoky blue fire, he stepped back.

"I'm taking you home now. Because if I don't, I doubt you'll ever see the place again."

He drove her car, brushing aside her protests with a careless "I'll grab a cab back."

Before they were halfway to her apartment, Helen was having trouble keeping her eyes open. Numb with fatigue, she finally gave up the battle and allowed her lids to drop, block out the hurtful glare from the headlights of the approaching cars.

"Where should I put the car? Do you have a designated space, or can you park anywhere?"

Marsh's quiet voice nudged her eyelids up. The car was motionless, the engine idling, at the entrance to the covered parking area adjacent to her apartment building.

"What? Oh, anywhere. It doesn't matter."

Even fuzzy-minded Helen could not miss the indulgent expression on his face. A smile curving his lips, he set the car in motion and drove onto the parking lot.

Too tired to argue, Helen simply shrugged when he insisted on seeing her safely into her apartment.

While she hung her coat in the closet, Marsh used her phone to call for a cab to pick him up. Standing by the door, she watched him cradle the receiver, then walk to her, a tingle of apprehensive anticipation growing stronger with each step he took.

"I won't be able to see you tomorrow or Saturday." He stopped in front of her, his tone regretful. "I have previous commitments that I can't break without causing friction on the homefront."

"Marsh, you don't have to explain your actions to me." Helen was experiencing that trapped, panicky feeling again. "You owe me nothing."

He smiled, raised his hand to caress her face, then went on as if she hadn't said a word.

"I'll be bored out of my gourd, but I can't get out of it without hurting my mother's feelings. But I want to spend the whole day with you Sunday—if you're free."

The feather-light touch of his fingers on her cheek set off a chain reaction along her nervous system. Her breathing growing shallow, she murmured, "Yes, but—"

"Out." Laughing softly, he shook his head at her. "I'll take you out somewhere. I'll pick you up in the morning at . . . ?" He lifted a questioning eyebrow.

"Not too early," she sighed, too tired to argue with him. "Unless I have a call, I sleep late on Sunday."

"Ten?"

Helen shivered with weariness, nodded.

"Okay." Feeling her shiver against his fingers, his eyes grew sharp. "Don't eat, we'll start the day with breakfast or brunch. How does a walk in the park sound?"

"In January?"

"Of course." He laughed again. "You'll see."

His eyes moved over her face, clung for a moment on her mouth, then came back to her eyes.

"You're exhausted, love. Go to bed and go to sleep. Don't think. Don't speculate. Block everything out and sleep."

His thumb stroked the dark smudges under her eyes as he lowered his head to hers and said softly, "I love you, Helen."

His lips, though firm, held no passion, no demand. Comforting warmth spread through her, easing the beginning ache at her temples. All too soon the warmth was removed, as moving away, he opened the door, murmured, "Sleep well, love," and was gone.

CHAPTER 4

Sunday dawned bright and cold. The end of January sunlight, glittering fiercely through Helen's bedroom windows, warned her not to go outdoors without her sunglasses.

Yawning hugely, stretching luxuriously, Helen glanced at the clock on her nightstand and gave a small yelp. Marsh would be arriving in less than an hour and here she lay, basking in the sun like a fat house cat. Scrambling out of bed, she grabbed her robe off the end of the bed and ran into the bathroom.

Helen felt good. Surprisingly she'd slept well the last few nights, including Thursday. She hadn't expected to, in fact, after Marsh had left her with his murmured, "Sleep well, love," she'd been convinced she wouldn't sleep at all. Contrarily she was asleep not three minutes after her head hit the pillow.

With two deliveries, plus the usual number of office patients, on Friday, and several hours in the operating room on Saturday, she'd tired herself enough to sleep on those two nights. The thought of Marsh, and what had happened in his bedroom, she'd managed to push to the back of her mind by concentrating fiercely on her work.

When, at the odd moments, the thought of him, the

remembered feel of him, crept to the forefront of her mind, she'd gritted her teeth, fighting down the shakiness that assailed her. Afraid, and unwilling to examine exactly why, she'd silently battled against the memories, using sleep as an ally.

Her door chimes pealed at exactly ten o'clock. Fastening the belt to her slacks, Helen walked to the door and pulled it open, her breath catching at the sight of him. He was dressed for a day out of doors in brown corduroy slacks, tan heavy knit sweater, and a fur-lined, high-collared parka.

Before she could speak, he dipped his head and placed his cold lips against hers.

"Good morning," he murmured, his breath fresh and tickly on her lips. "May I come in?"

"Yes—yes, of course." She stepped back to allow him to walk by, then added hurriedly, "I'm ready to leave. All I have to do is put on my coat."

A grin slashed his mouth, revealed perfect white teeth. His eyes danced with gentle mockery.

"Although I'll admit to being tempted, I'm not going to jump on you and drag you into the bedroom, Helen, but"—his arm shot out, snaked around her waist, pulled her to him—"I am going to kiss you properly."

As he lowered his head his hands came up to cup her face, cool fingers sliding over the smoothed back hair above her ears.

"Marsh! Don't you dare touch those pins."

Laughter rumbling in his throat, the tip of one finger gently nudged the curved metal hair anchor back into place under the neat coil.

"Spoilsport."

The word was murmured against her lips, which, unbidden, had parted to receive his. Several inches separated him and Helen, yet he made no move to get closer, as if deliberately denying his body the feel of hers. His hands on her face, his mouth on hers, was their only physical contact, yet Helen felt a warmth and security flow through her that could not have been stronger had he enfolded her in his arms, held her tightly against his strong, hard body.

When he lifted his head, she had to bite back the soft cry of protest that rose in her throat. Opening her eyes, she felt her breath cut off altogether at the intensity of his blue gaze. The fingers of his right hand trailed slowly down her cheek, over her lips, then with a sharp shake of his head he stepped back, a rueful smile twisting his mouth.

"I think we'd better get out of here," he clipped tersely, going to the closet to get her coat.

Shaken, Helen stood mutely, automatically lifting her arms to the sleeves of her coat when he held it for her. When his hands dropped away from her shoulders, she found her voice.

"I must stop at the hospital."

"Why?"

The sharp edge to his tone drove the fuzziness from her mind. The face she lifted to him was cool, composed.

"I must make my rounds. I have three post-op and four maternity patients to examine and release papers to sign for another—" Helen paused in midsentence, a look of concern shadowing her eyes. "Marsh, the patient being released this morning is your sister."

"I know that." One dark brow went up in question. "So?"

"Well—I—mm—I mean." Helen faltered, then asked quickly, "Were you planning to wait for me in the car?"

"Hell, no!" He snapped irritably. "Do you know how cold it is out there? And I sure as hell didn't consider wasting gas to keep the car warm. If you don't want me trailing around behind you, leave Kris till last and I'll visit with her while you make your rounds."

"But—" Helen hesitated, her fingers playing nervously

with her coat buttons. "Marsh, what will your sister think?"

"Who cares what she thinks?" He pulled the door open angrily. "Now, can we go and get these rounds over with? I'm hungry."

An uneasy silence rode with them all the way to the hospital. By the time Marsh stopped the car at the entrance, Helen's nerves were ragged.

"I'll park the car and see you later in Kris's room."

Helen chose to ignore the anger that still laced his tone. She didn't want him to wait for her in his sister's room, simply because she didn't want Kristeen Darren to know that they were together.

"Why don't you wait for me in the lunchroom? Have some toast and a cup of—"

"Helen!" he exploded. "Will you get on with it? At the rate we're moving it will be lunchtime before we get breakfast."

Hot anger shot through her, and not bothering to reply, she slammed out of the car and into the building. *I must be out of my mind,* she fumed. *Why did I agree to spend the day with him? Did I, in fact, actually agree?*

Thoughts of the same nature seethed in her mind as Helen made her rounds, her cool outward appearance giving no hint of the anger that boiled in her veins. Not since Carl had she allowed a man to upset her like this. And the fact that he was younger than she was an added thorn. She was doing the work she loved and was completely satisfied with her life. She didn't need any man, let alone a smooth-talking rich kid who could issue orders like a marine sergeant.

By the time she walked into Kristeen Darren's room, Helen was in a cold fury and ready to tell Marshall Kirk to go to hell. The scene that met Helen's eyes as she walked through the doorway brought an abrupt halt to her angry stride.

Kristeen was sitting on the bed fully dressed, an impatient frown on her face. Her husband paced restlessly between the room's only window and the bed. Her mother sat, back rigid, in a chair beside the bed. And in the corner, sitting on a functional, straight-backed chair, Marsh somehow managed to look lazily comfortable. Helen's eyes slid over him as if he were not there.

"I'm sorry I'm late, Kristeen." She apologized briskly, drawing four pairs of eyes to her. "I've signed your release, and they'll be bringing your baby to you in a minute. How are you feeling this morning?"

Her fingers on Kristeen's wrist, her eyes on her watch, Helen smiled and nodded understandably at the young woman's breathless tone.

"I'm fine, Doctor. Excited about taking my baby home."

"Of course," she murmured, adjusting her stethoscope. Satisfied with what she heard, Helen glanced at Kristeen as she removed the instrument. "Okay, you may go. Do you have any questions about the instructions I gave you yesterday?"

"No, Doctor, everything's clear."

"Fine. If you have any problem whatever, call my office." Except for the cursory glance she'd given him on first entering the room, Helen had not looked at Marsh. She did not look at him now as, smiling warmly at the other three, she wished Kristeen good luck with her daughter, said she'd see her in six weeks, and turned to leave. Marsh's voice stopped her a foot from the door.

"Helen."

The sound of her name in that smooth, too-soft tone sent a chill along her spine. Turning slowly, she met his eyes, her breath catching at the mocking slant of his lips, the flash of blue fire in his eyes.

Out of the corner of her eye Helen caught the confused glances that flew between Kristeen, her husband, and her mother. Using every ounce of willpower she possessed, Helen hung on to her cool.

"Yes?"

"You're finished now?"

Helen's teeth ground together at the warm note Marsh had inflected into his voice. Just what did he think he was doing? she thought furiously, noting the sharp glance his mother turned at him. Her tone went from cool to cold.

"Yes."

"Then, my love, can we now go and have breakfast? My stomach is beginning to feel divorced from the rest of my body."

The soft gasps that came from the two women, the low whistle that Mike Darren emitted, grated against Helen's nerves. She could have happily hit him. Instead she nodded her head sharply and turned to the door. He was beside her before she had taken three steps, his arm sliding possessively around her waist.

"Take care, Kristeen," he said lightly, shepherding Helen out of the room. "I'll see you all later."

Too angry to trust herself with words, Helen maintained a frigid silence as she retrieved her coat and followed him to his car. Spitting like an angry cat, she turned to him as soon as both car doors were closed.

"Damn you, Kirk," she began heatedly, only to have him cut her off with a soft warning.

"Watch it, my sweet. I'll take just about anything from you, except your cursing me."

"I'm not asking you to take anything at all from me," she sputtered, growing more angry by the minute. "And I want nothing from you. Not a meal, or a walk in the park, or your company. I'm going home."

Helen turned to the door, hand groping for the release, and gave a sharp cry of pain when his hands grasped her shoulders, pulled her around to face him.

"You're not going anywhere," he growled, giving her a not-too-gentle shake. "At least not until you tell me what you're so mad about."

"Oh, I'm not mad, Mr. Kirk." Helen returned his growl. "I'm way past mad. Try furious. Better yet, try incensed."

"But why?" His confusion was unfeigned. As angry as she was, Helen had no doubt of that. For some reason it incited her even more.

"Why?" She choked. "Why? What were you trying to do back there in Kristeen's room? Do you know?"

"Yes, I know," he replied evenly. "I was determined to make you acknowledge my existence. You would have walked out of that room without even looking at me, wouldn't you?"

"Yes," she answered bluntly.

"Yes," he repeated grimly. "And that's why I stopped you."

"And because I bruised your delicate ego, you mentioned our having breakfast together in a tone that suggested we spent the night together."

"Oh," he breathed out slowly. "Now we get to the real reason for your anger. You didn't want anyone—not just my family, but anyone—to know we were together because you were afraid they'd wonder if we were sleeping together. That's why you wanted me to wait in the car or lunchroom."

"Exactly." Helen's face had taken on her cool, withdrawn, professional expression. Her tone held frigid hauteur. "My reputation, both professionally and privately, is spotless. I fully intend to keep it that way. I will not have my name bandied about in speculative gossip."

The laughter that met her stilted statement wiped the composure off Helen's face.

"Bandied about?" he gasped, between whoops of delight. "Oh! I love it. Bandied about." With an obvious effort he brought his roars under control. "You straight-backed screwball. Where did you pull that chestnut from?"

Against her better judgment Helen felt her lips twitch with humor. What a pompous ass she sounded. Where had she pulled that chestnut from?

"Don't laugh at me, Marsh," she scolded quietly. "It's not polite to ridicule your elders."

Hot, swift anger wiped the amusement from his face, cut off the laughter still rumbling in his chest. The abrupt transition startled and frightened her.

"Damn you, Helen," he snarled softly, fingers digging painfully into her shoulders. "What is this stupid hang-up you have about our ages? You are not my *elder*." Helen's eyes widened as his face drew close to hers. "You will not speak to me as if I were a naughty boy." His eyes glittered with intent, robbing Helen of breath. "A naughty man maybe, but not a naughty boy."

His lips, hard with anger, forced hers apart. The rigid tip of his tongue flicked against her teeth, stirring an unwanted curl of excitement in her midsection.

"You want a taste of the man, Helen?"

A seductive whisper, then his mouth crushed hers hungrily, his tongue plunged to extract the sweetness as a bee extracts honey from the blossom.

Helen's heart seemed to stop, then the beat increased to thunder in her ears like the hoofbeats of a wildly galloping horse. Good Lord! It was the last coherent thought she had for several seconds. His hands turned her, pushed her gently against the seat, and her breasts were crushed by the weight of his chest.

An ache began, deep inside, that quickly grew to enormous proportions. Giving in to the need to get closer to him, Helen's arms encircled his waist, tightened convulsively.

His mouth left hers reluctantly, came back as if unwilling to have the moment end. Between slow, languorous forays, he muttered, "How long, Helen? How long before you face reality and yourself? You want me. I know you do."

Helen brought her hand up, her fingers moving across his lips.

"Marsh, stop." Her breathing was uneven, erratic. "I

don't want any emotional involvements. Oh, Marsh, please." His lips were busy against her fingers, his teeth nipped playfully. "There's no time in my life for a man."

"Too late," he murmured. His lips caught the tip of her ring finger, sucked gently. "You've got a man in your life. At the moment a very hungry man." He moved away from her, back behind the steering wheel, a rueful smile slanting his mouth. "A hungry man in more ways than one. Are we going to go eat or are you going to sit there and watch me slowly starve to death?"

Helen welcomed his return to humor with a sigh of relief. Although his anger had been brief, it had been fierce and he had really frightened her. What would he be like, she wondered fleetingly, if he really let loose? She could only hope she never had to witness it, let alone be the cause of it. The mere thought made her feel cold all over. Shrugging to cover the shiver that shook her slim frame, Helen gave in.

"All right, Marsh, you win. We'll go eat."

His smile grew into a rakish grin. "At the risk of sounding conceited, I think I'd better warn you that I usually do. Win, that is."

Later, sitting in a small restaurant, Helen toyed with her cheese omelet and watched, fascinated, while Marsh demolished a huge club sandwich and double order of French fries. Their conversation had been minimal as he attacked the food like a man who was actually starving.

When he finished, he wiped his lips with his napkin, indicated to the waitress that he'd like his coffee cup refilled, sat back, and turned that unnerving blue gaze on her.

"Are you from Philly originally?"

Helen blinked with the suddenness of his question after the long silence. Nodding to the waitress who held the coffee pot paused over her cup, her eyebrows raised questioningly, Helen matched his casual tone. "No, I was born up near Wilkes-Barre. My father was a G.P., had a surprisingly large practice considering the size of the community."

"Was? Had?" He probed.

"He retired two years ago. He and my mother sold everything and moved to Phoenix, Arizona." She lifted her gaze from her coffee cup, unaware of the touch of sadness he could see in her eyes, the wistfulness of her small smile. "I miss them."

"Of course." His voice lost some of its casualness. "You have other family here? Brothers, sisters?"

"No." She shook her head. "I have a younger brother, he's also in Phoenix. That's the main reason Mother and Dad decided to retire there. He, Rob, has two small children. My parents wanted to watch their grandchildren grow up." Helen's smile twisted wryly. "They gave up the hope of seeing any grandchildren from me a long time ago."

"Why?" Marsh's tone sharpened. "You're not too old to have kids."

Helen breathed deeply, lit a cigarette with surprisingly steady hands. "I don't want children, Marsh."

His eyes narrowed at the calm finality of her tone. Frowning, he reached across the table, slid a cigarette from her pack, lit it, then exhaled in a soft sigh. His shoulders lifted, came down again in an oddly resigned gesture.

"Okay." His tone was flat, but steady. "We won't have any."

"Won't have any! Marsh—"

Helen stopped herself on hearing her own rising voice. She glanced around quickly before continuing in a much lower, fiercer tone. "Marsh, what are you talking about? You know my feelings on—"

"Not here." Marsh rose, silencing her effectively. In the car she turned to him as soon as he'd slid behind the wheel. "Not here, either," he snapped with finality.

Helen was amazed at the number of people in Fairmont Park. It was very cold and the wind, though not strong, bit at her exposed skin with icy teeth. "Incredible," she murmured, after they'd been walking for some minutes. "Is it like this every Sunday?"

"Yes." He slanted a mocking glance at her. "Helen, I find it hard to believe you didn't know. Don't you ever watch the local news on T.V.?"

"I rarely watch T.V. at all." She replied, glancing around interestedly. "I did know the park was a favorite spot for joggers but I had no idea there were this many people into jogging, let alone all these other people here."

"You live a rather single-minded existence, don't you?" he chided.

"I never thought of it that way, but"—she shrugged—"I suppose I do. Which reminds me. Back at the restaurant you said— Marsh! What are you doing?"

He had taken her gloved left hand in his larger bare one. After tugging her glove off, he laced the fingers of his right hand through hers, then slipped their clasped hands into the deep fur-lined slash pocket of his jacket. When she tried to pull her hand free, his fingers tightened until she cried out in pain. "Marsh, please."

"Stop fighting me." His fingers loosened, but not enough for her to slip free. "And back at the restaurant I said that if you didn't want children we wouldn't have any."

He was so unconcerned, so nonchalant, Helen was beginning to feel she'd get better results talking to one of the park's many trees. Fighting to hang on to her patience, she gritted slowly.

"That's right, *we* won't have any chillren. *We* won't have anything together for the simple reason we won't be together. What do I have to do to make you understand? I don't want a relationship. I don't want to be bothered by any man." During this entire tirade Helen's tone had not risen above a harsh whisper. Now she drew a ragged breath and added in a more normal tone, "Do I make myself clear?"

"Perfectly."

It was what she'd wanted to hear, so why did his prompt, careless answer cause a sharp pain in her chest? No sooner had the thought skittered through her mind than he added blandly, "There's only one problem, my love. You are already bothered by a man. This man. And this man plans to bother you one hell of a lot more before he's through."

"Marsh," Helen began angrily, but he cut in in that same bland tone.

"Let's shelve the subject for now and enjoy our walk. Are you cold?"

"Yes. No. A little." Helen could have shouted at him, he had her so frustrated, she didn't know what she was saying. And his soft, delighted laughter didn't help much either. "I mean I am a little cold but I'm enjoying the walk."

"Good. Do you want to walk down to the river and see if there are any hardy souls crewing?"

Helen hesitated. If there were boats on the river, she'd like to see them. But then again, her nose was beginning to feel numb now and the wind off the water would be a lot colder, so she shivered and shook her head. "I don't think so. Another day perhaps."

"Chicken." He taunted softly. "Don't tell me you're a hothouse flower."

"Coming from Wilkes Barre?" She laughed. "You have got to be kidding. Why, when I was in the sixth grade I was the undisputed snowball champ."

"Liar."

Helen's laughter sang on the cold air, bringing a bemused expression to his eyes, a deepening timbre to his voice. "What were you really like in sixth grade?"

"Quiet, studious, head-of-the-class type. You know." She paused, looked away from him. "I never wanted to be anything but a doctor. My mother despaired at my nose in a book, but my father was delighted. He had similar hopes for Rob too, but Rob had his own ideas." She laughed again, a soft, reminiscent laugh. "Rob's a charmer. Always has been. He could talk the face off an eight-day clock. A born salesman. And that's exactly what he is. Makes an excellent living at it too."

"You miss him." It was not a question. "Were you very close?"

"Yes." Helen closed her eyes against the sudden, sharp longing she felt for her distant family. "While we were growing up we fought like a dog and cat. Nearly drove my mother mad. Our saving grace was that we also defended each other fiercely against outsiders." She laughed again at a particular memory.

"Tell me," Marsh prompted. "Let me share the laughter."

"It's silly." Helen shook her head, still smiling. "To this day Rob tells people that I was named Laura, after my mother, but I grew up a hell-en and it stuck."

"You *do* miss him." Inside the pocket his fingers squeezed hers, sending a shaft of exciting warmth up her arm. "When did you see him last?"

"I flew out for a week last spring for his birthday." She frowned, remembering. Her tone lost its sparkle, went flat. "His thirty-first. I've always thought of Rob as my baby brother, Marsh, and he's a year older than you are."

A tautness came into his body. She could feel it in the arm that rested against hers, in the tightening of his fingers. "Do you think of me in the same vein?" Even his voice was taut.

"Marsh, I—"

"Do you?" Harsh now, rough, he stopped walking, turned to face her.

"No." It was a shaken whisper, but she could not lie to him with that intent blue gaze on her. His deep sigh formed a misty cloud between them.

"It's a damned good thing," he grated. "Helen, unless you want to see some real fireworks, I think you'd better make a concentrated effort to forget the difference in our ages. Without too much prodding I could become positively paranoid about it."

He leaned closer to her and his voice went very low. Not in self-consciousness of the people passing by, but in sheer intensity. "I love you, Helen. I don't know *how* I know, but I *do* know that if there were ten or even fifteen years between us, I would still love you."

"Marsh, I—I—" Shaken by his declaration, unsure, Helen searched for words.

"Leave it for now," he said softly. The bone-crushing grip on her fingers was eased as the tension went out of his body. "We came here to walk, let's walk."

They had taken only a few steps when he jiggled her fingers, and requested, "Tell me some more about your family."

"No." The eyes that met his sharp look were teasing. "Tell me about yours. I'm curious to know what type people it takes to produce such a—a—"

"Bonehead?" he suggested dryly. "Bulldog? Bast—"

"Marsh!"

His head was thrown back in laughter. Joyful, enchanting laughter that stole her breath, doubled the rate of her heartbeat. And before she realized what he was doing, he turned, bent his head, and caught her mouth with his, unconcerned with the giggles that came from a group of teen-age girls passing by.

Helen felt as gauche as a teen-ager herself, feeling her cheeks grow hot when he lifted his head, grinned at her, and whispered, "I do love kissing you."

"You're a fool," she whispered back, trying to sound stern, failing miserably.

"Yes, well, we'll go into that another time," he warned. "But now"—he resumed walking again, totally relaxed—"my family. My mother's beautiful, as I'm sure you noticed." He raised dark brows at her and she nodded. "My father's rich, and I mean old guard, Society Hill, rich.

Kris is a pet. She used to be a drag, trailing after me all the time, but even when she was a drag, she was a pet. I love them all, but I adore my grandfather."

Helen looked up quickly, breath catching at the softness in his tone, his eyes. The strong lines of his face, the russet hair, those incredibly clear blue eyes, were becoming too familiar, too heart-wrenching important. In an effort to shake off her thoughts, Helen prompted, "Your grandfather?"

"Yes." He smiled. "My grandfather. You'll like him," he stated emphatically. "And I know he's going to be crazy about you." He laughed softly at some secret joke, then went on. "My grandfather is definitely not old guard. A real scrapper still, and he's close to seventy-five. Chews me out regularly, enjoys every minute of it too. He started sixty years ago with a couple of hundred dollars, which was all that was left after his father died, and built it into a small empire. It keeps me running, trying to handle the damn thing."

"Started what?"

"A small building and construction firm that is now a very large building and construction firm, plus assorted other interests he's picked up along the way."

"So you do work for a living," she chided. "I did wonder. You're a construction worker?"

"Among other things." That devastating grin flashed. "My father wanted me to follow him into banking." He grimaced. "Can you see me as a banker?" Helen smiled, shook her head. "Yeah, well, neither could I. Cullen couldn't either."

"Cullen?"

"My grandfather. I've called him Cullen, on his insistence, for as long as I can remember. Drove my grandparents on my father's side up the wall."

"Cullen is your mother's father."

"Yes. Her mother died giving her life and although Cullen wanted a son, he never remarried. He told me there wasn't a woman alive who could replace his Megan. Anyway, after she died, he lived for his work and his daughter. I think he claimed me for himself about five minutes after I was born. My father didn't stand a chance against the old bear."

"Your father gave in to him without a fight?" Helen asked incredulously, thinking of the battle anyone would have had trying to claim her brother away from her father.

"Hell, no." Marsh chuckled. "Dad's no slouch. The tug-of-war lasted through all the years I was growing up, with me in the middle, catching flak from both sides."

They had retraced their steps back to the car and Helen was glad to slide onto the velour-upholstered seat, out of the cold air. She waited until he'd started the car and drove into the flow of traffic before observing, "I'm surprised you weren't scarred by the war. Or were you?"

"It wasn't that kind of war." He stopped at a stop sign and turned to give her an encompassing glance. "You look frozen. Any warmth coming from the heater yet?"

"Yes, a little, but I'm fine." Helen turned to study his features. "What kind of war was it?"

"Friendly. Dad and Cullen get along fine, always did. I suppose you could say they fought their battle like a chess game, only I was the only chessman. One would move me this way, the other another way."

"And your grandfather made the deciding move?" Helen couldn't decide if she was fascinated or appalled by the story.

"No." Marsh grinned. "I did."

"But, Marsh, you said earlier that you ran the business, that must mean your grandfather got what he wanted."

"You think so?" he taunted softly. "Ask him sometime."

Helen had been so caught up in watching the play of emotions on his face, she hadn't once glanced out the window. When he drove the car into a small parking area, she looked around in confusion. The parking lot was adjacent to a small Italian restaurant in a part of the city she was unfamiliar with. Her eyes came back to him as he turned the key, cutting the engine.

"Why are we stopping here?"

"This is one of my favorite haunts. I'm addicted to their shrimp scampi." Her widening eyes brought the grin back to his mouth. "I walked off my lunch," he defended himself carelessly. "I'm hungry." His eyes went over her face, dropped to her slim wrists. "Some good, rich Italian food wouldn't hurt you either. Were you always so thin?"

"Oh, for heaven's sake," Helen groaned, reaching for the door release. "You sound like Alice."

He was out of his door and around to hers in time to close it for her. "Who's Alice?"

"My office nurse."

"Oh, yes, the dragon I talked to on the phone Thursday." He held open the door into the restaurant for her to precede him inside, and as he helped her with her coat he asked wryly, "Does Alice look as daunting as she sounds?"

"And as bossy." Helen nodded. "She has been nagging me for weeks about my weight."

"I think I like Alice," he murmured as a tall, swarthy man approached, a huge smile revealing glistening white teeth.

"Hiya, Marsh, haven't seen you for a while." His bold, dark eyes slid over Helen appreciatively. When his eyes returned to Marsh they held a trace of envy. "Where've you been hiding out, *compare?*"

Marsh put his hand out to clasp the other man's, a taunting grin curving his lips. "Not hiding, Moe, working. Cullen's had me on the run for weeks."

Moe looked at Helen, letting his glance linger deliberately a second before remarking, "Not too much on the run. You've obviously had time for other things. Very beautiful other things."

Marsh laughed aloud, and Helen couldn't help smiling back at the good-looking Moe. He was about the same age as Marsh, with black curly hair, dark brown eyes, and a sexy look about him that probably ensnared women in droves.

"Helen, this smart-mouthed Sicilian is Emilio Brenzini, Moe to you. He's the owner of this joint. He's also my best friend, I think." Marsh turned a sardonic face to Moe. "Moe, Helen Cassidy. Doctor Helen Cassidy, my future wife."

Helen's shocked gasp was covered up by Moe's shouted, "What? Hey, man, that's terrific. Come and sit down." They were ushered to a small table covered with a blood-red cloth, matching napkins folded neatly beside carefully arranged flatware. When Moe moved behind Helen to hold her chair, she glared at Marsh, who smiled back sweetly. Choking back the angry words she wanted to spit at him, she forced a smile to her lips when Moe was again facing them.

"I just can't believe it," Moe exclaimed in awe. "Marshall Kirk, man about town, heartbreaker extraordinaire, brought down in his prime by a female sawbones." His eyes glittered at Helen. "What the hell did such a gorgeous creature as you see in this big number-counting lady killer?"

"Knock off the comedy routine, Moe," Marsh drawled. "And break out the wine. Helen and I were outside for hours and we need some warming up."

"Okay, sweetheart." Moe did a bad imitation of Bogart and walked away, chuckling to himself.

The moment he was out of sight Helen snapped, "How dare you tell him that."

"Why not?" Marsh answered blandly. "You are going to be my wife."

"No, I am not." She gritted furiously. "Do you understand? I am not. When Moe comes back, you tell him you were joking."

"No."

"Marsh, I'm warning you." Seething, Helen had trouble enunciating her words. "If you don't tell him, I will."

Marsh eyed her dispassionately. "Have fun," he drawled. "But personally I think you're going to sound pretty damned silly. Moe's going to wonder why you didn't deny it at once."

Helen opened her mouth, closed it again, trying to collect some control. Then Moe was back, grinning happily as he poured the ruby-red wine.

"To both of you." He lifted his glass, his face sobering as he turned to Helen. "I should say I hope you'll be very happy but with this one"—he jerked his head at Marsh, a soft smile touching his lips—"I don't really think it's necessary. He is the best there is, Helen. Only a very foolish woman would not find happiness with him." Then he turned to Marsh, glass going high in salute.

"Congratulations, *compare*. I begin to suspect that you are a very, very lucky man."

CHAPTER 5

Sleep eluding her, Helen lay on her back, staring at the pale white ceiling. It was late, several hours since Marsh had left, and yet her mind hung on to the day's happenings as tenaciously as a baby monkey hangs on to its mother.

She had said nothing to clarify the situation to Moe, of course. How could she after the sincerity of his toast to them?

Positive she'd choke if she tried to force food around the anger waiting to explode from her throat, Helen had surprised herself by not only eating but keeping pace with Marsh. The scampi was every bit as delicious as Marsh had claimed, but then, the antipasto, tossed salad, large slices of crispy crusted bread, and spumoni were the best Helen had ever eaten also. When they had drained the last drop of wine and were preparing to leave, Marsh reached for his wallet. Moe placed his hand on Marsh's arm and shook his head.

"This one's on me, buddy. Bring Helen over to meet Jeanette soon." He laughed softly before adding, "They've already got one thing in common."

At Helen's questioning look Marsh explained, "The medical profession, love. Jeanette is an anesthetist."

"Really? Where?" Those were her first unstrained words since Marsh had told Moe she was to be his wife. Moe named the hospital and Helen smiled, nodded. "Yes, I'm familiar with it. They have excellent facilities and a first-rate staff. Does she enjoy her work?"

"Most of the time." Moe's answer was laconic. "Sometimes it all gets on top of her. You know, the job, taking care of the kids, the house"—he grinned—"keeping me happy."

Curious, Helen asked, "How many children do you have?" His smug answer shocked her.

"Four. Five years of marriage and four *bambinos*. That's pretty good work, wouldn't you say, Doc?"

"Four babies and she keeps up the pace in O.R.?" Helen returned incredulously. "Moe, you are married to a superwoman."

"Jeanette *is* a super person," Marsh put in, edging her to the door. "But don't think for a minute this buffoon doesn't take good care of her. She works by choice, and she has plenty of help in the house. The *gran signore* here gets his masculine ego kicks by giving people the impression he's got a master-slave marital arrangement. When in fact he'd drop onto his knees and kiss the hem of her uniform if she asked him to."

"Without hesitation" was Moe's emphatic response.

Even now, hours later, Helen shook her head in wonder at Moe's wife. A date had been set, for the following Saturday, for Helen and Marsh to join Moe and Jeanette for dinner at the restaurant. Helen was looking forward to meeting her.

When, finally, they had left Emilio's, Helen had withdrawn into a cold silence. Marsh had not made an attempt to break that silence, although he had cast several searching glances at her.

Helen was mad, and she wanted him to know she was

mad. She simmered with indignation all the way home, while he parked the car, rode up in the elevator with her, stood behind her as she turned the key in the lock. When she turned to give him a frosty good-night, he reached around her, pushed the door open, spun her around, gave her a gentle shove, and followed her into the room. Eyes blazing, she'd whirled back to face him. He beat her to the draw.

"Okay, you're mad." His voice was low, steady, unrepentent. "So let's have it. Get it out of your system and then we'll talk calmly about it."

"I don't want to talk about it," Helen said coldly. "You will have to make my apology next Saturday night. I am not going with you. I do not want to see you again. I do not want you to call me." Breathing deeply, she stared into his impassive, expressionless face. "Is that understood?"

"You're nuts, do you know that?"

The soft, taunting amusement in his tone drew a gasp from her. Before she could form words of retaliation, he stepped in front of her, grasped her shoulders, and gave her a light shake.

"For all your cool, self-contained act, it doesn't take much to set you off, does it?" His eyebrows arched and a knowing smile twitched his lips. "Or is it me?" he chided softly. "I have a hunch that if any other man had made that statement, you would have, very coolly, called him a liar." His voice went softer still. "I get to you, don't I? I rattle you and ruffle your feathers. I make you mad, but"—he lowered his head to within an inch of hers—"I can also make you laugh." His mouth brushed hers, once, twice. "But what really bothers you is that I excite you." The tip of his tongue slid across her lips, parting them in a small, involuntary gasp. His mouth covered hers, his hands moved down her spine, molding her against him.

At first she struggled against him, clenching her teeth

and jaw tightly. But what he said was true. He did excite her, and that excitement curled around and through her, loosening her jaw, weakening her knees, driving her arms up and around his neck to cling helplessly while his mouth plundered hers.

Helen moved restlessly on the bed. Just thinking about him sparked off that excitement, sent it scampering wildly through her body. The words he'd whispered against her lips now brought a low moan from her throat.

"I want to sleep with you, Helen. Let me stay. Let me exorcise, once and for all, the fears that have kept your emotions frozen all these years." He pulled her closer, his arms tightening. His breath danced across her ear. "Trust me, love, I won't hurt you."

"No, no."

Her words had a desperate, panicky sound, even to her own ears, and he allowed her to move out of his arms, away from him. He watched her pull the ragged edges of her composure together, then he sighed softly and walked to the door.

"I'll call you tomorrow."

"Marsh, I said—"

"Damn it, Helen," he flared, "don't fight me. Do you want me to come back over there? Prove to you that there's a woman inside that cool, professional veneer you've covered yourself with?"

She backed away warily, shaking her head in answer.

"All right then, play it cool for a while, see what develops. Now," he sighed again, impatiently, "what's the best time to call you tomorrow?"

"After six thirty. Here."

Why had she given in to him? Helen silently asked her ceiling. Why did she let him brush aside her protests as if they meant nothing? Her mouth twisted in self-mockery. Maybe, because, if she was honest with herself, they meant exactly that: nothing.

Helen went rigid, fingers curling lightly around the bedcovers. The self-truth was a shocking jolt her stiffened body tried to reject. *Face it, Dr. Cassidy,* she told herself derisively, *you're as human and vulnerable as the next woman. You like the breathlessness that intent, blue gaze causes. You like the feeling of weakness the touch of his hand on your body induces. You like the crazy riot of sensations his hungry mouth generates. For the first time in over ten years you have a physical need for a man. But why this particular man?*

Helen's mind darted in different directions in an effort to avoid answering her own question. It was quite true she'd felt no urges of a sexual nature since the night of Carl's assault. Filled with disgust, contempt, she had, for many months, withdrawn from any kind of personal contact with the opposite sex. As time passed and circumstances demanded she have some contact with men, the contempt lessened, and in a few cases was replaced by respect and admiration, but that was all. It was as if the part of her brain that controlled her emotional responses had closed shop—permanently. With the rest of her mind she could evaluate a man's potential and his accomplishments, and applaud them, but always as a contemporary, never, ever, as an interesting male.

Now, suddenly, this one man, this *younger* man, was arousing all kinds of needs and wants inside her.

"No, please." It was a whispered cry into the room's darkness. The stiffness drained out of her body, replaced by a longing ache that made what she'd felt for Carl, before *that* night, seem mild and insipid by comparison.

Head moving from side to side on the pillow, Helen's eyes closed slowly. After all these years the emotional control center in her brain was alert and functioning and sending out signals she could not deny. She wanted this man. She needed this man. *Damn it to hell,* she thought furiously, *I'm in love with him.*

No! I can't be, her reason rebelled. *I don't even know him and I never even found out what it is, exactly, he does. Then, irrelevantly, he's not even in the medical profession.* The irrationality of her thoughts struck her, and aloud she moaned, "He is right, I am nuts."

The bedcovers twisted around her squirming body as she fought against the insidious languor thoughts of him had produced. *I am not in love,* she told herself firmly. *Of course I'm not. This—this craziness is just that: physical craziness. Marsh is a good-looking—no, handsome— man. He has charm, and money, in abundance, and face it, he is downright sexy.* His eyes alone had the power to set off a chain reaction of sensations inside a woman. *And,* she rationalized, *I can surely handle my own physical attraction to him. I must. I cannot, I will not, expose myself to that kind of pain again. I'm a mature woman, not a silly young girl. And I certainly will not be an object of any man's pleasure. Most especially a young man.*

Helen winced. Why, when all the mature, sophisticated men she'd met had left her cold, did she react so strongly to him? His assertion that they were fated to come together she dismissed as nonsense. She was a physician. She was aware, if not fully understanding, of the age-old mystery of one person's chemistry striking sparks off of another. But it was totally incomprehensible to her why his was the only chemistry able to ignite hers, after all this time. She would not have it. She had worked too hard to allow a man, probably going through a phase in which he was attracted to older women, to disrupt her life.

For a long time Helen's thoughts ran on in the same vein, always coming back to the same conclusion. Since she could not order him to stay away—he paid no attention to her when she did—she'd go along with him, keeping him at arm's length, until the phase, or attraction, wore itself out.

Finally the plaguing ache left her body and she relaxed, grew drowsy. Her last coherent thought was he could not hurt her if she simply refused to allow herself to *be* hurt.

She held on to that thought all through office hours the next day, whenever Marsh invaded her mind. She was in the apartment not fifteen minutes when the phone rang. Going to the wall phone in the kitchen, Helen glanced at the clock, thinking it must be her service as Marsh was not due to call for a half hour.

"Dr. Cassidy." She spoke briskly into the receiver.

"I don't want to speak to Dr. Cassidy," the low voice taunted. "I want to speak to Helen. Is she there?"

Steeling herself against the warmth the sound of his voice sent racing through her body, Helen asked coolly, "Is there a difference?"

His soft laughter sent a shiver after the warmth. "A very big difference," he stated firmly. "Dr. Cassidy is a machine, Helen is a woman."

Stung by his jibe, surprised at the swift shaft of pain it caused, Helen murmured, "That wasn't very nice, Marsh."

"When did I ever say I was nice?" he mocked. "Oh, I have my moments, but not with you. I don't want to be nice to you. What I want to do is shake some sense into your rigid mind. But not tonight. I'll have to pass on that pleasure for the rest of the week." He paused and his tone took on an edge Helen didn't understand. "I'm going out of town for the rest of the week. I must make a circuit of several of my clients, clear up a few things." Now he sounded annoyed, as if angry at the claim to his time. "The damned incompetence of some bookkeepers today is not to be believed." Again he paused, and his tone had a controlled, frustrated ring. "I'll be back sometime Friday. I'll call you."

"All right, Marsh." Helen's calm reply gave away none of the confusion she was feeling. After wishing him a safe trip and hanging up the receiver, Helen moved around the kitchen, getting herself something to eat, her mind nagging at his tone.

Why had he been so annoyed? she wondered with a vague twinge of unease. After forcing down a cold sliced roast beef sandwich and a small salad, she brewed a pot of herb tea and carried it into the living room. As she sipped the hot, green liquid Helen speculated on the reason for his anger. Was it really caused by the need to visit clients or was it connected in some way with her?

Cup in hand, Helen moved restlessly around the tastefully decorated room in a vain attempt to escape her thoughts. It didn't work. Her thoughts pursued her as she paced back and forth, into the kitchen to wash up her few dishes. He had been angry the night before. Angry and impatient and very likely frustrated with his failure at getting her into bed with him.

A shudder rippled through her body and she stood unmoving at the sink, the towel she'd been drying her hands on hanging forgotten in her fingers. Had he thought she'd be an easy conquest? Her behavior the previous Thursday may have led him to believe so. Did he think, like many other people, that an unmarried woman in her mid-thirties was so desperate for male companionship that she'd hop into bed with almost any male?

Wincing, Helen tossed aside the towel and went back to pacing the living room. Unlike most women, reaching thirty, thirty-five, had not bothered her. Why should it? She was performing at the peak of her efficiency and she knew it. She lived well and had a comfortable sum of money in the bank. Her life was evolving as planned. What more could she possibly ask for? Up until now her answer to that would have been an emphatic nothing. But now the answer that shouted in her mind shook her with its intensity.

She wanted Marsh. She wanted the feel of his mouth on hers, his arms tight around her, his body, hard and urgent, leaving her in no doubt that he wanted her as badly.

Becoming tired, yet unable to sit still, Helen continued to pace in a nervous, jerky manner that in itself was alien to her usual smooth movements. She did not feel like herself. She wasn't even sure what she did feel like. She didn't like it, but wasn't quite sure what to do about it.

Maybe, she decided clinically as she prepared for bed, she should have an affair with him, get him out of her system, let him get her out of his. She toyed with the idea a moment, then rejected it. No, she could not do that, for she felt positive that in an encounter or affair like that she would end up wounded if not crushed. While he, malelike, would blithely walk away, one Helen Cassidy forgotten, looking for new battlefields to conquer. No! She wasn't quite sure how she'd handle the situation, but she felt positive that if she played along with him, let him have it all his way, she'd be the one left torn and bleeding on this particular battlefield.

So ran her thoughts for the remainder of the week, and by the time her alarm rang on Friday morning she was thoroughly sick of them. Although it was an extremely busy week, with several deliveries and her office packed with patients, it had seemed like an endless one.

By the time her last patient left on Friday afternoon, Helen decided she'd been a fool to give the matter so much consideration. Without Marsh's proximity she had reached the point of observing the whole affair objectively and came to the conclusion that she was mountain climbing over molehills.

Her sense of balance restored, Helen went home with the conviction that she could handle one Marshall Kirk with one hand tied behind her back. Her right hand at that.

She would, she thought smugly, do exactly as Marsh had recommended: play it cool. She would go with him to have dinner with Moe and his wife and start the evening with a flat denial of Marsh's assertions of the previous Sunday.

Helen waited for his call until after midnight, her hard-fought balance slipping away as each hour died a slow death. And when, in the small hours, she did finally drift into an uneasy sleep, she felt actually bruised, as if she'd been beaten, and her pillow knew an unfamiliar dampness.

Her phone rang before her alarm, and as she had two patients due at any time, Helen snatched up the receiver on the second ring.

"Good morning, love, did I wake you?"

Marsh's soft voice sent an anticipatory shiver through Helen's body, and she had to clutch the receiver to keep from dropping it. How, she wondered, did he manage to sound so seductive at this hour of the morning.

"Yes." And why did she have to sound so breathless and sleepy?

"I could tell," he purred sexily. "You sound warm and cuddly and"—he paused—"ready, and I wish like hell that I was there right now."

Helen's mouth went dry, and she placed her hand over the receiver as if afraid he could actually see her wet her lips.

"No comeback?" Marsh taunted softly. "No cutting reply? You must still be half asleep." He laughed low in his throat. "Or is it the other? Are you all warm . . . and so forth?"

The jarring noise of her alarm broke the spell his sensuous voice had caught her up in. So much for firm resolutions and objective reasoning, Helen thought wryly, her finger silencing the alarm's persistent ring.

"Actually." How had she achieved that detached tone? "I was confused for a moment as to who it was. It's been so long since I heard your voice." A gentle, but effective, reminder that he'd said he'd call the night before.

His laughter appreciated the thrust. "You lie so convincingly, darling. Is it one of your habits?" His laughter deepened at the half gasp her covering hand was not fast enough to blank out entirely. "I know I said I'd call you last night but it was very late when I got in and I didn't want to disturb you—or did I manage to do that anyway?"

The soft insinuation brought a sparkle of anger, self-directed, to Helen's now-wide-awake hazel eyes. Biting back the few choice names she would have found much pleasure in calling him at this safe distance, she snapped waspishly, "Marsh, I have to go to work. Did you call for a reason or just to annoy me?"

"Ah-ha, she's awake now, and the transformation has been made. There speaks the mechanical Dr. Cassidy."

"Marsh, have you been up all night?" Helen enunciated with exaggerated patience. "You sound somewhat light-headed."

"It's an affliction that attacks the minds of men when they're in love," Marsh replied seriously. Then he added wickedly, "And have the hots."

"Not men," she retaliated harshly. "Callow youths."

"Mind your tongue, Helen." The bantering tone was gone, replaced by steel-edged anger.

"Marsh, it's after seven thirty." Helen retreated quickly. "I have to get ready for work. What, exactly, did you call for?"

"To find out what your early-morning voice sounds like," he shot back smoothly. "And to tell you I'll pick you up at seven."

"All right, now I must go."

"And, Helen? Give me a break and let your hair down. Bye, love."

Fuming, Helen stood several seconds, listening to the

dial tone before replacing the receiver, unsure if he had meant her to take his request literally or figuratively.

The morning went surprisingly well and before one thirty Helen found herself free for the day. About to leave the office, she turned back, picked up her phone, and called the hairdresser who occasionally cut and styled her hair. Yes, the young woman told her, if Helen could come right in, she could work her in.

When she let herself into her apartment several hours later, Helen's hair had been shampooed, shaped, and blown dry. It lay in soft curls and waves around her face and against her shoulders.

Later, as she was putting the finishing touches to her makeup, Helen paused to study the unfamiliar hairstyle. At first, the change being so radical from her usual smoothed-back neatness, Helen had not been sure if she liked it. But now, after living with it for some hours, she had to admit that the loose curls and waves framing her face softened the stubborn line of her chin, the curve of her cheek. Was she, perhaps, past the age for such a careless style? Her hazel eyes sharpened, searched thoroughly, but the thick mane, not quite brown, yet not quite blond, revealed not a sign of gray. Well, maybe for the weekends, the rare evening out, she finally decided. But never, never for the office, the hospital. The one thing she didn't want while she was working was to appear, in any way, softened or vulnerable. At one minute to seven Helen stepped out of the elevator into the apartment building's small lobby and came face to face with Marsh. Without speaking, she watched his eyes widen, flicker with admiration and approval as they went over her hair, her face, then move down to the muted red of her wool coat. She could actually feel the touch of that blue gaze as it slowly traveled the length of her slim, sheer nylon-clad legs to her narrow feet, not at all covered by the few thin straps of her narrow-heeled sandals. When he raised his eyes to hers, Helen felt her heartbeat slow down then speed up into an alarmingly rapid thud. The expression in his eyes, on his strong, handsome face, was so blatantly sensual, all the moisture evaporated from her mouth and throat.

"You are one beautiful woman." His voice was very low, yet each word was clear, distinct. "Why in the hell do you ever pull your hair back off your face?"

Helen stared at her own reflection in his eyes, suddenly filled with an overwhelming desire to lose herself in their blue depths. Her lips parted, the tip of her tongue skimming over them wetly, but no words came. She heard him draw in his breath sharply, saw him lift his hands, take a step toward her before he brought himself up abruptly, a rueful smile twisting his lips.

"We had better get out of here, love," he murmured hoarsely, "before I do something that would very likely delight the people in this lobby but embarrass you."

With that he stepped beside her, grasped her elbow, and hurried her toward the front entrance. It was only then that Helen became aware of the group of people in the lobby, laughing and talking about the evening ahead, calling a greeting to another couple as they came in the door and joined the group.

As they passed the group several pairs of eyes turned in their direction, and Helen could not help but see the sharp looks of interest and appreciation. Avid female glances took in Marsh's imposing figure; warm male eyes ran over her own.

With a jolt Helen realized that up until that point she and Marsh had been unobserved and that the eternity that had seemed to pass while she'd stared into his eyes had, in actuality, lasted only a few brief seconds.

Oddly shaken, Helen walked beside him in silence to the car, slid obediently onto the seat as he held the door. Her mind numb, refusing to delve for any deep meaning in the incident, Helen stared through the windshield as Marsh slid behind the wheel, started the engine, and drove away from the parking lot.

When the stunned sensation left her, Helen stole a glance at Marsh's set profile. Her glance froze and held for long seconds before, with a smothered gasp, she forced her eyes back to the windshield. But the windshield couldn't hold her gaze, and slowly, almost against her will, her eyes crept back to fasten hungrily on his face. She had not realized how very much she'd missed him. In something very close to pain her eyes devoured the sight of him, soaked the image of him into her mind, her senses.

"Stop it, Helen."

Helen blinked at the raw harshness of his voice, stammered, "W—what?"

"You know damn well what," he rasped. "I can *feel* your eyes on me. We have a date with Moe and Jeanette, but if you don't look away, I'm going to say the hell with it, turn the car around, and take you to my place."

"Marsh—I—" Helen began tremulously.

"I mean it, Helen." He cut across her words roughly. "The way I feel right this minute, I could park this car at the first empty spot I find and make love to you and not give a damn if we drew an audience."

A shiver of excited anticipation slid down Helen's spine, then shocked at her reaction to his threat, she practically jumped away from him and glued her eyes to the side window.

"That's better." His tone had smoothed out and it now held amusement. Helen gritted her teeth and a few moments later greeted with a sigh of relief the bright red neon sign that spelled out the name EMILIO'S.

There was an awkward stiffness between them as they left the car and walked to the restaurant, but the awkwardness soon dissolved when exposed to the sincere warmth of Moe's greeting. With unrestrained pride Moe drew his wife forward to introduce her to Helen.

At a quick, cursory glance Jeanette may have appeared simply pretty. But, as Helen's glance was neither quick nor cursory, she was struck by the beauty of Jeanette's mass of short, shiny black curls, her wide, dark brown eyes, which somehow managed to look both femininely soft and sharply intelligent at the same time.

With a flourish Moe ushered them to a table, telling them menus wouldn't be necessary as he and Jeanette had completely planned the meal from appetizer to dessert. When a small wiry waiter walked up to their table carrying a silver bucket containing a bottle with a foil-wrapped head, a happy grin spread across Moe's face.

"For my *compare* and his beautiful bride-to-be"—his hand grasped the neck of the bottle, lifted it to reveal the Dom Pérignon label—"nothing but the best."

In frozen silence, a strained smile cracking her pale face, Helen heard the muffled pop of the cork as it was forced from the bottle by Moe's hand, hidden beneath a towel. Watching the golden liquid as it cascaded, bubbling, into the tulip-shaped glasses, Helen thought frantically: *Now is the time to speak, put an end to this pretense.*

In cloying panic she had the uncanny feeling that if she did not speak before the toast was given she'd be trapped into a situation from which she'd never get free. *That's ridiculous,* she told herself scathingly, casting about in her mind for light, joking words that would correct Marsh's statement of the week before without putting a damper on the party. She knew, already, that she was going to really like Moe and Jeanette and she didn't want to begin a friendship with a lie.

Unable to find the proper words, Helen's mind went blank. The glasses were passed around, and Moe and Jeanette lifted theirs. Surprisingly it was Jeanette who offered the toast. Her smile, her entire face, revealing the affection she felt for him, she looked directly at Marsh.

"To our favorite man, who deserves the best." She then looked at Helen, drawing her into the circle of affection. "And to his woman, who obviously is."

"*Bravissimo, cara,*" Moe applauded as he lifted his glass to his lips.

"*Grazie,*" Marsh replied simply before leaning across the table to kiss Jeanette's smiling mouth.

Self-schooled to show as little emotion as possible, Helen had listened to the toast, observed Marsh's reaction to it, and stared openly as the two men embraced each other, with a growing sense of wonder. Did these people always display their feelings this openly? Then all conjecture was sent flying as Moe's amazingly gentle lips touched hers. Startled, about to pull back and away, Marsh's chiding voice saved her from making a fool of herself.

"Enough already, you greedy Sicilian. It's my turn."

The gentle lips were removed, replaced by an equally gentle pair. And yet there was a difference. A difference so electrifying, Helen felt the shock waves reverberate through her entire body. He must have felt it too for he lifted his head too swiftly, breathed, "Later, love," and turned a smiling face back to Moe and Jeanette.

The toast over, Helen relaxed and, before she was even aware of being drawn, found herself laughing and talking with Moe and Jeanette as if she'd known them for years. The minute they'd finished their after-dinner liqueur and coffee, Moe stood up, his grin directed at Marsh.

"Come with me, *paesano*, I got to show you my new ovens."

Marsh rose but stood still when Jeanette placed a staying hand on his arm. Turning to her husband, she sighed exaggeratedly, "Marsh doesn't want to see your ovens, Moe."

Moe's eyes, as soulful as a scolded cocker spaniel, shifted from Marsh to Jeanette, then back to Marsh.

"Tell the heartless woman you want to see my new ovens, Marsh," he pleaded petulantly.

His lips twitching, Marsh stared into Jeanette's laughing brown eyes and said seriously, "I want to see Moe's new ovens, heartless woman."

Jeanette's carefully controlled features dissolved into laughter. Waving one hand dismissively, she cried, "Oh, for heaven's sake, go admire the new ovens, you two lunatics."

Shaking her curly black head, Jeanette turned back to Helen with a grimace that quickly turned into a smile. "I swear, sometimes I think that man loves his kitchens more than he loves me."

"Kitchens?" Helen queried.

"Yes," the black head nodded. "He has three restaurants, even though this place, being the first, is his favorite."

"Does he do any of the cooking?"

"Lord, yes!" Jeanette exclaimed. "Here and at home. And what a cook!" She placed closed fingertips to her lips and kissed them. "I have to starve myself during working hours or there would be a lot more of me."

"Well, if he cooked tonight's dinner," Helen said laughingly, "I can understand your problem."

"You know, Helen." Jeanette's tone went low, serious. "When Moe came home raving about Marsh's beautiful woman, I thought, yeah, just another in a long line of beautiful women. But five minutes after we met, I knew you were not just a beautiful woman in any man's line. You're special, and that makes me happy, because Marsh is also special and his happiness is very important to Moe and me."

What could one possibly reply to a sentiment like that? Feeling anything she'd say would be vastly inadequate,

Helen nevertheless began an attempt to tell Jeanette the truth.

"Jeanette, I don't know quite how to say this, but—"

"By your solemn expression, love," Marsh inserted, "I have a nasty suspicion my best friend's wife has been telling tales out of school."

"Every chance I can," Jeanette retorted. "We girls have to stick together if we hope to keep you guys in line."

The moment for taking Jeanette into her confidence was past, and Helen felt an odd relief at Marsh's interruption. Strangely she hated the idea of disappointing Moe and Jeanette.

CHAPTER 6

It was close to midnight before the party broke up. It seemed to Helen that they talked nonstop, one minute laughingly, the next seriously. There were even a few friendly arguments, which nobody won, ending happily with everyone agreeing to disagree. Helen amazed herself with her own participation. She couldn't remember the last time she'd entered into a free-for-all conversation so effortlessly, and she enjoyed every minute of it.

When the last of the other dinner patrons had left, Moe, Marsh, and a few of the waiters cleared a small area of floor space by moving several tables together, and Moe found some slow, late-night music on the stereo-FM radio behind the bar.

He then came to Helen and, with a courtly, old-world bow, requested the honor of the first dance. Moe was a good dancer; in fact he was the next thing to expert. Never very proficient herself, Helen found it hard to relax. When the music ended and was followed immediately by another, slower, number, Helen swirled out of one pair of arms into another.

Although he moved smoothly, evenly, Marsh was not nearly as expert as Moe and as his steps were less intricate, Helen followed his lead easier. As one song followed another and the tension of concentration seeped out of her body, Marsh's arms tightened. His steps grew slower until, locked together, they were simply swaying to the music, oblivious of the knowing smiles of Moe and Jeanette, the shadowy movements of the waiters as they unobtrusively cleared the tables.

On the way home, still in a mellow mood, Helen tipped her head back against the headrest and softly hummed one of the tunes they'd danced to.

"You like my friends?" Marsh's quiet tone blended with her mood, and she answered without hesitation.

"Very much."

"I'm glad." He was quiet a moment, then added softly, "Maybe you'll introduce me to some of your friends sometime."

The mood was shattered, and Helen sat up straight, alert and wary. Now she did hesitate, for although his voice was soft, his tone had tautened.

"Maybe," she said, hedging, "sometime."

His soft laughter mocked her but he didn't pursue the subject. Instead he taunted, "Did you miss me this week?"

"Why?" Helen asked blandly, innocently. "Were you away?"

This time his laughter filled the car, scurried down her spine.

"That'll cost you also," he purred warningly. "You are racking up quite a bill, woman. And I fully intend to make you pay in toto."

"I don't have the vaguest idea what you're talking about." Helen managed a light tone, despite the lick of excitement that shot through her veins.

"Oh, I think you do," he mocked. "Now answer my question. Did you miss me?"

"Well, maybe a little." She returned his mocking tone. "Like one might miss a persistent itch after it's gone."

"Deeper and deeper," he said, chuckling. "You're going to need a ladder to get yourself out of the hole you're digging."

He parked the car on the lot close to the building and grinned when she turned to say good night.

"Save your breath, I'm coming up with you."

"But, Marsh, it's late and—"

"Save it." He cut her off. "I'm coming up with you, Helen. That almost kiss I got early this evening wore off long ago. Besides which, I thought you'd offer me a nightcap or at least a cup of coffee."

"Coffee! At this hour?"

"You forget, I'm still young," he teased roughly. "Coffee never keeps me awake. Now stop stalling and let's go."

They went, Helen at an irritated, impatient clip, Marsh at a long-legged saunter beside her. She only glanced at him once on the way up. One glance at his twitching lips, his blue eyes dancing with devilry, was enough to send her blood racing—with anger?—through her body.

Inside the apartment she flung her coat and bag onto a chair and stormed into the kitchen. His soft laughter, as he carefully hung up her coat, crawled up the back of her neck, made her scalp tingle.

She was pouring the water into the top of the automatic coffee maker when he entered the room, and after sliding the glass pot into place, Helen turned, eyes widening. He had not only removed his topcoat, but his jacket and tie as well, and had opened the top three buttons of his shirt. Turning away quickly, she pulled open the cabinet door, shaking fingers fumbling for cups. Damn him, she thought wildly, trying to concentrate on getting the cups safely out of the cabinet. *How can I hope to keep him at arm's length when he's already half undressed? And how in the world do I handle a man that simply laughs at me and refuses to be handled? More to the point, how do I handle myself when I know that what I want to do is finish the job he started on his shirt, feel his warm skin against my fingertips?*

Angry with him, with herself, with everything in general, she slid the cups from the shelf and banged them onto the countertop. Glaring at the coffee running into the pot, she snapped, "Make yourself at home."

"I intend to."

She hadn't heard him move up behind her, and she jumped when his arms slid around her waist, drew her back against him. When his lips touched her cheek, she cried, "Marsh, the coffee's ready."

"So am I," he murmured close to her ear, his hands moving slowly up her rib cage. "God, I missed you," he groaned. "You may only have missed me like the absence of an itch, but this is one itch that is going to persist until you have to scratch. Helen."

Helen's mouth went dry and her eyes closed against the sigh of urgency he put into her name. She gasped softly when his teeth nipped her lobe, then her eyes flew wide as his hands moved over her breasts.

"Marsh, stop."

Her words whirled away as she was twirled inside his arms. His hungry mouth, covering hers, allowed no more words for several moments. Feeling her resolve, her determination, melt under the heat of his obvious desire, Helen pushed at his chest, head moving back and forth in agitation.

"Marsh, the coffee."

"The hell with the coffee," he growled harshly. "Helen, I've barely thought of anything but this all week. Now will you be quiet and let me kiss you?"

"No." She pushed harder against his chest. "Marsh, you—you wanted the damn coffee and you're going to drink it or you're going to go home."

He sighed, but his hands dropped to his sides. "All

right, I'll drink the coffee." He gave in, then qualified. "If you'll join me."

The room crackled with tension as she filled the cups, placed them, along with cream and sugar, on the table. Sitting opposite him, sipping nervously at the brew she didn't want, Helen could feel the tension like a tangible presence. When he spoke, the calm normalcy of his tone struck her like a dash of cold water.

"Were you very busy this week?"

"Yes."

Try as she did, she could not come up with any other words. The silence yawned in front of her again, and her head jerked up when he blandly asked, "What's that you say? Did I have a busy week? As a matter of fact I did." His eyes bored into hers. "Even though I seemed to spend as much time in the air as on the ground. Altoona, Harrisburg, Pittsburgh."

He stopped abruptly, his eyes refusing to release hers. But he had achieved his purpose, he had reignited her curiosity about his work.

"Your grandfather's building and construction firm extends throughout the state?"

The blue gaze softened and he smiled.

"No, but he does have business interests not only throughout the state but along the entire East Coast."

"I see."

Helen sipped her coffee, then stared into the creamy brew. She really didn't know any more than she had before. When she looked up, she was caught by the waiting stillness about Marsh, the hint of amusement in his eyes. *He's not going to volunteer a thing,* she thought frustratedly. *He's going to sit there, silently laughing at me, and make me ask. The hell with it,* she fumed, *and him. I don't even care what he does.*

With elaborate casualness she got up, walked to the counter, and refilled her cup with coffee she wanted even less than the first cup. When he held out his cup to her, his lips twitching, she refilled it and handed it back to him, fighting down the urge to upend it over his head. She was going to ask. She knew she was going to ask and she resented him for it. Why was it so important to her anyway? The less she knew about him the better. Right?

"Do you handle all your grandfather's interests?" Well, at least she'd managed an unconcerned tone, she congratulated herself.

"Mostly," he replied laconically. "But I wasn't on Cullen's business this trip. I was on my own."

Helen glanced up hopefully, but he was calmly drinking his coffee, his eyes mocking her over the cup's rim. *Damn him,* she thought furiously. *Why is he doing this?* "Because he knows," reason told her. *He knows how much I hate this need to know everything about him. God, can he read my mind?* It was not the first time she'd wondered about that, and the idea, as ridiculous as it was, made her uneasy. Placing her cup carefully in the saucer, Helen sighed in defeat.

"What is your business, Marsh?"

"Now, that hardly hurt at all, did it?" Marsh mocked softly. Then all traces of mocking were gone, but the amusement deepened, danced in his eyes. "I'm an accountant."

"An accountant!"

At her tone of astonished disbelief his laughter escaped, danced across the table and along her nerve ends. "An accountant," he repeated dryly. "Don't I look like an accountant?"

"Hardly." Helen had control of herself now, her dryness matched his. "Does King Kong look like a monkey?"

"Do I look like King Kong?" His laughter deepened and Helen felt a strange, melting sensation inside. Her own eyes sparkling with amusement, she answered sweetly, "Only when you're angry."

He was up and around the table before Helen even finished speaking, and still laughing, he pulled her out of her chair and into his arms.

"You want to play Fay Wray?" He grinned suggestively.

"To an accountant?" Helen taunted.

"Ah, but you see, love," he said in the same suggestive tone, "accountants know all about figures." His hands moved slowly down her back, over her hips. "And you've got one of the best I've ever handled."

"And you've handled so many?" Helen shot back, annoyed at the twinge of pain the memory of Jeanette's words about Marsh's women sent tearing through her chest.

"Enough," he admitted lazily. His arms tightened, drawing her close to his muscle-tautened frame. "Helen," he murmured urgently. "You're driving me crazy." His mouth was a driving force that pushed her head back, crushed the resistance out of her.

Feeling her body soften traitorously against him, Helen sighed fatalistically. She *had* missed him. She had missed *this*. Her hands, imprisoned between them, inched to the center of his chest. She heard his sharply indrawn breath when her fingers began undoing the buttons still fastened on his shirt, and when she paused, heard him groan, "Good God, love, don't stop."

His lips left a fiery, hungry trail down her arched throat; his hands moved restlessly over her shoulders, her back, her hips. His lips back tracked to the sensitive skin behind her ear. His voice was a hoarse, exciting seducement. "I love you. I love you. It's been such a long week. Helen, don't send me home, let me stay with you."

"Marsh, oh, Marsh." Helen could hardly speak. Her breath came in short, quick gasps through her parted lips. The shirt was open and she felt him shudder when her fingers tentatively stroked his heated skin.

"More, more." His mouth hovered tantalizingly over

hers. Her hands pushed away the silky material of his shirt as they slid up his chest, over his shoulders. With a low moan his mouth crushed hers in a demand she no longer could, or wanted to, deny.

The ring of the wall phone, not three feet from Helen's head, was a shrill intrusion of reality. It was a call she couldn't ignore, and on the second ring she struggled against him. Cursing softly, Marsh released her reluctantly.

With shaking hands Helen grasped the receiver, drew a deep breath, and huskily said, "Dr. Cassidy."

"Sorry to waken you, Doctor," the voice of the never-seen person who worked for her service said apologetically. "I just had a call from a Mr. Rayburn. He said his wife's labor pains are ten minutes apart and she's spotting, and he is taking her to the hospital."

"Thank you." Helen's husky, sleepy-sounding tone had brisked to wide-awake alertness. Without even looking at Marsh, she swung through the doorway to the living room, calling to him over her shoulder, "Marsh, you may as well go home. I have to go to the hospital and I have no idea how long I'll be."

He caught up with her halfway across the living room, grasping her arm to spin her around to face him.

"I'll drive you and wait for you."

Impatient to be gone, Helen shrugged his hand from her arm. "Don't be silly! I told you I have no idea how long it will take. It's one thirty in the morning. Go home, get some sleep."

"But I don't mind—"

"Marsh, please," Helen interrupted sharply. Cold reality, and the knowledge of how close she'd come to sharing her bed with him, put an edge on her tongue. "I have to go and I want to change my clothes. Will you just go home?"

"Would you object if I wait while you change and walk

down to your car with you?" Marsh asked sarcastically. "As you said, it is one thirty in the morning."

"Oh, all right," Helen replied ungraciously, turning to run into the bedroom.

When she came hurrying back a few minutes later, he was standing at the door, holding her coat and handbag.

"Marsh, I—I'm sorry I was so sharp with you," Helen apologized haltingly, sliding her arms into the sleeves of her coat. "It's just that I . . . well—"

"Don't worry about it." His hands tightened a second on her shoulders before he removed them and turned to open the door. "Had you scared for a minute there in the kitchen, didn't I?" he teased as she walked by him into the hall. His good humor was entirely restored and the devil gleam was back in his eyes.

"I don't understand." Flustered, Helen stepped into the elevator, then turned deliberately widened, questioning eyes to him.

"You understand perfectly," he said softly, tormenting her. "I'm going to get you and you know it. It's just a matter of time." He paused, grinning ruefully. "And an uninterrupted opportunity."

As they stepped out of the apartment entrance, for the second time that night, they were met by a swirl of snowflakes.

"I hope this doesn't amount to anything." Marsh frowned, looking up at the dirty gray sky.

"Why, don't you like snow, Marsh?" Helen had always liked snow.

"As a rule it doesn't bother me one way or the other," he answered, taking her keys from her fingers as they reached her car. He unlocked the door, handed her keys back, then opened the door for her and added, "But tonight, at who knows what time, my girl's going to be driving home in it, so I hope it doesn't amount to anything."

Amii Lorin

Before she could say anything he kissed her hard on the mouth and strode across the lot in the direction of his car, parked some distance away.

His girl! His *girl!* Helen wasn't sure if she was amused or angry. His girl indeed. As she drove off the lot Marsh's car was two bright headlights reflected in her rearview mirror. And the reflection was there, every time she glanced in the mirror, all the way to the hospital. Now she was sure she was angry.

After parking her car in the section marked DOCTORS ONLY, Helen flung out of the car and across the lot to where the big Lincoln sat idling quietly. He slid out of the car when she reached the front fender. Walking with jerky, angry steps around the door, she snapped, "What do you think you're doing? I asked you to go home."

Without a word he pulled her into his arms, kissed her roughly.

"And I'm going home," he grated when he lifted his head. "I wanted to make sure you got here safely, and to tell you to call me when you get home."

"But I don't know what time it will be." She started walking toward a side entrance, Marsh close beside her.

"That doesn't matter," he stated flatly.

"Marsh, I do this all the time," Helen reasoned.

"And people get stopped and attacked in their cars more and more all the time." His tone was adamant, final. "Helen, I mean it. Promise you'll call or I'll wait right here."

"All right, I promise." Helen yanked open the door. "Now will you go and let me get to the delivery room before that baby does?"

"Okay, I'll go. Don't forget."

Helen was gone, practically running down the long hall to the elevators.

It was a hard delivery and Helen felt exhausted when she finally let herself into her living room close to three thirty. At least she hadn't had to face treacherous driving conditions, as the snow squall had moved off and the streets were dry.

The baby was a large one and had taken quite a bit out of his mother, not to mention Helen. Like a sleepwalker she went into the bedroom and undressed, thinking light-headedly that even at birth most males gave woman an undue amount of trouble. After washing her face and hands, Helen sat on the side of her bed, lit a cigarette, and picked up the phone.

"Helen?" Marsh's voice questioned after the first ring.

"Yes, Marsh." Helen spoke softly, tiredly. "I'm home."

"You sound beat, love. Was it bad?" Deep concern laced his tone.

"For a while there," she sighed. "But Mrs. Rayburn is fine and so is her son and I'm half asleep sitting here."

"I can hear that," he murmured. "I wish I was there to hold you, reward you. Go to bed, love. I'll call you tomorrow afternoon. By the way, my parents would like you to come for dinner tomorrow, or should I say tonight, but I'll tell you more about that when I call. Good night, love."

Helen murmured good night, replaced the receiver, then sat up with a start. His parents' for dinner! Whatever for? Good grief! Was she to be brought home to Mother and Dad for approval? Was Marsh out of his mind to think she'd stand for that? And what did he mean by reward me?

Too many questions in a mind too tired to search for answers. Helen crushed out her cigarette, switched off the light, crawled into bed, and was instantly asleep.

The phone remained considerately silent all Sunday morning, and Helen slept until after noon. She was glancing over the paper, sipping at her second cup of coffee, when the instrument issued its insistent cry. It was Marsh, and she was ready for him.

"What was all that business about dinner at your parents' home?" Helen began the moment he'd finished saying, "Good morning, love, did you sleep well?"

There was a long pause, then he asked smoothly, "Are you always this prickly when you first wake up?"

"Only when I've been sent to sleep with the threat of being paraded for approval, like a horse at an auction," she replied acidly.

"Only with the very best Thoroughbred fillies, darling." He laughed softly. "What gave you the idea you were going to be paraded?"

"It smacks too much of 'bring the girl home for inspection before you do anything stupid, son,'" Helen retorted. "Really, Marsh, why else would they invite me?"

"Because they want to meet you? Get to know you?" His amusement curled along the line to her.

"Why now? All of a sudden?" she asked bluntly.

"All right, Helen." His voice sobered, grew serious. "I admit that Mother asked a few discreet questions after we left Kris's room together. I'm also sure she had already talked to my father about it, as he was there during the"—he paused—"questioning."

"And?" Helen prompted.

"I told them I'd asked you to marry me."

The calm statement almost had the power to curl Helen's hair.

"Marsh, you didn't!" Helen fairly screamed into the mouthpiece.

"Don't fall apart, love." He was laughing again. "I was honest. I told them you'd turned me down—for now."

"Marshall Kirk," Helen gritted, "if you're trying to get yourself strangled, you are going about it in the right way. I can't go."

"You'd better," he warned. "I've told them we'll be there at seven. It won't be all that bad, love. Kris and Mike will be there, and as an extra added attraction they've invited Cullen. You can sit back and watch my father and the old bear take verbal potshots at each other."

Good Lord, the whole family! Helen groaned. *Am I going prematurely senile? I must be or I wouldn't put up with this silliness. Why should I volunteer to endure this meet-the-family routine? I haven't the slightest intention of getting involved with him in any way, let alone marry him.* The scene in that very kitchen the night before returned to mock her, and she groaned again.

"Helen? What's the matter?" His sharp query made her aware of how long she'd been quiet. His next question assured her he'd heard her soft groan. "Are you crying?"

"I never cry," she answered bitingly. "I don't have the time."

"But you *do* have time for dinner tonight." He bit back. "And I *will* come for you at six thirty." The bite turned into a threat. "And you'd *better* be ready."

Helen simmered, just below boiling point, all afternoon. Marsh's parting thrust, "You'd *better* be ready," stabbing at her mind like the tip of a red-hot poker.

You fool! she berated herself unmercifully. *You stupid fool! You have no sense at all?* Silently, as if to another person, she dressed herself down as harshly as a tough top sergeant might a raw recruit. *You, a professional— whose very pride is in that cool professionalism—are you going to meekly submit to the dictates of a man? What can you be thinking of? You are* not *a twittering teenager. You are* not *a fresh-faced young woman, just starting out. You have earned your pride, your confidence, your independence. And you did it by yourself, without the support, the consideration of any male.*

Although the day waned, Helen's self-directed fury did not. As she went about washing the few dishes in the sink, making her bed, straightening the apartment, her mental tirade continued.

Now, now when you've reached the point in life where

you hold that pride, that independence, tightly in your hands, are you going to fling it all away for the brief assuagement of your resurrected physical needs? And don't, for one minute, try to convince yourself it will be anything but brief.

At five forty-five, her soft lips twisted in self-derision, Helen stepped under the shower. Still scolding silently, she told her invisible target, *The very idea of a woman like you is a challenge to the Marshall Kirks of this world. He says he loves you. In all probability he would say or do anything to get what he wants.*

Helen stepped out of the shower, scooped up a towel, and began patting herself dry. *And what does he want, you ask?* Helen went still, a wry smile tugging at her lips as she gazed into the hazel eyes of the recipient of her condemnation, reflected in the full-length mirror on the back of the bathroom door. *Okay, you asked for it. I'll tell you exactly what he wants. He wants the power to make you come to heel, like a well-trained puppy, at his mildest command. He wants the exquisite satisfaction of knowing he has brought the very cool, so very professional, Dr. Cassidy to her knees. And when he is sated with that satisfaction, he will take a walk—and forget to come back. Are you willing,* Helen asked those watchful, reflected eyes, *to deny everything you've worked so hard for, for a few moments of mindless bliss that can only be found in this one man's arms?*

Helen blinked, and her head snapped up. The answer was there, in the clear hazel eyes staring back at her. Silently, yet loud and clear, those eyes proclaimed, "No way."

Her self-denouncement completed, Helen dressed slowly, carefully, a secret smile softening the contours of her face. She had tried, and failed, to convince Marsh of her disinterest in any kind of male-female relationship. He had, figuratively, backed her into a corner. She refused to cower in that corner. Her intelligent father and gentle mother had not raised a female fool. She would play Marsh's game, and beat him at it.

The doorbell rang at exactly six thirty. Composing her features, squaring her shoulders, Helen went to open the door, a smile of welcome curving her lips. The smile wavered at the sheer, overpowering look of him, then strengthened at the memory of her resolve.

He was dressed in a dark suit and silk shirt, which matched exactly the color of his eyes, and a patterned tie, which contrasted, yet complemented, his attire. The overall effect was one of elegantly covered, raw masculinity. His gleaming, not-quite red hair had been slightly tousled by the wind. His gray topcoat had been tossed carelessly over one broad shoulder, and his casually arrogant stance gave him the look of a well-dressed hell-raiser.

"Good eve—" He broke off midword, a stunned expression on his face, as his eyes made a slow tour of her body, while her own expression returned the compliment.

Without speaking, Helen moved back to allow him to enter, then closed the door quietly and turned to face him.

After long deliberation she had dressed in a long, narrow black velvet skirt with a snugly fitting matching vest over a smoky-colored, long-sleeved chiffon blouse. A single strand of milky-white pearls (a gift from her brother when she had graduated from medical school) glowed around her slender throat. The warm admiration in his eyes told her she'd chosen well.

"Black on black," he murmured when her eyes met his. "Very effective with your hair, your fair skin, and the pearls." His voice deepened huskily. "You're beautiful, Helen."

A thrill of excitement shot through Helen, followed by a shaft of elation. He had called the game and dealt out the cards on the day they met. Now, she decided, was the time for her to pick up her hand and play her first card.

Helen's eyes lifted to his. "Thank you. You—you're beautiful too." She laughed softly. "I suppose a woman shouldn't tell a man he's beautiful, but you are, you know. A beautiful male animal."

A flame ignited in his eyes and he drew his breath in very slowly. As he exhaled, equally slowly, he moved to stand close to her.

"I don't know if a woman is suppose to tell a man that," he murmured. "But I know this man likes hearing it." His hands came up to cup her face. "Tell me more. Tell me why you think I'm beautiful."

"I don't know if I can explain, exactly." Helen searched for words. "Certainly you are very attractive, but you know that. You dress well. Instead of simply covering your body, your clothes enhance it, proclaim your masculinity."

His thumb moved caressingly over her cheek, and Helen paused to run her tongue over suddenly dry lips.

"An invitation if I ever saw one," he whispered, bending his head to touch his mouth to hers. "Is there more?" he whispered against her lips.

"You make me laugh, even when I'm angry," Helen whispered back. "And you make me breathless, most of the time."

"Are you breathless now?"

"Yes."

"And me." His mouth crushed hers, sending the room spinning around her head.

When he lifted his head and the room settled back into place, Helen drew deep breaths to calm her racing senses. "Marsh, we must go, your parents are expecting us."

"I know," he groaned. "Helen, will you let me stay?"

It was time to play the second card. Lifting her hand to his face, she trailed her slim fingers across his cheek, over his firm lips. "Marsh, please, be patient with me. Let me get to know you, feel . . . easier . . . with you. It's been a long time since I've felt safe with a man." She shuddered and felt his lips kiss her finger. "I don't want what happened that night in your apartment to happen again." She slid her hand from his mouth, across his face, and around his neck to draw his head close to hers. Her lips against his, she pleaded, "Please, Marsh."

Helen felt a ripple run through his body and heard his soft sigh before he answered tersely, "All right, love, I won't pressure you. But I think it's only fair to warn you that I want you very badly and I'm going to do every damned thing I can think of to warm that core of ice that's deep inside you."

He stepped back, his eyes eating her, then he shook his head and muttered, "We'd better leave."

CHAPTER 7

Helen shivered, but not from the outside cold. The warmth from the car's heater protected them from the biting winds and subzero temperature. The soft music from the tape deck added to that warmth. The chill was inside Helen, deep inside. The shiver stemmed from two different sources. One of them was excitement, the other, fear. The elements of both those emotions had Helen at near-fever pitch.

The feeling of power that had surged through her at Marsh's reaction to her small advance had generated an excitement Helen had never experienced before. It was heady, exhilarating, while at the same time, she realized, a little dangerous. And then there was the tiny fear that had begun with Marsh's words. Taken at face value they were innocuous enough. But could she take them at face value? There was the seed of her growing fear. *"I'm going to do every damned thing I can think of to warm that core of ice."* A simple straightforward promise? Or something more? Perhaps she was reading words between the lines that simply were not there, but his tone, everything about him, had been so intense that a small alarm had sounded inside her mind.

"You're very quiet," Marsh said softly into her thoughts. "You're not nervous about meeting the family, are you?"

All traces of his earlier intensity were gone, and telling herself she was being overimaginative, Helen turned to him with a smile.

"A little," she admitted. "Mostly of your grandfather. He sounds a very formidable character."

"Oh, he is that." Marsh laughed. "But he's a pushover for a beautiful woman. And an absolute lapdog for one with intelligence as well as beauty. You, love, will have him eating out of your hand fifteen minutes after you're there."

"Your confidence in my feminine prowess is overwhelming," Helen murmured dryly, secretly elated. He thought she was beautiful. He thought she was intelligent. She was a challenge to his manhood, and he wanted to overcome that challenge by possessing her physically. *Nothing very complicated or scary about that,* she assured herself. *You, Doctor, have been chasing shadows that just are not there. Relax and enjoy the game until the final card is played.*

Marsh's parents' home loomed large and imposing, the many brightly lit windows a beacon in the winter-night darkness. From the moment she stepped inside the door Helen could feel the wealth and good taste of its owners surround her. The family, the very correct butler informed Marsh, were in the small rear sitting room. Following his ramrod-straight back across the wide hall, Helen chanced a glance at Marsh and received a slow, exaggerated wink in return.

The small rear sitting room was not really at the rear and not small at all, and very, very elegant. Helen judged that the furniture, paintings, and exquisite decorations in the room had probably cost more than she could earn if she worked flat out until she was ninety. A room definitely not for small children, she thought, wondering if

Marsh and his sister had been barred from it while they were growing up.

Marsh's mother, a tall, attractive woman in her midfifties, came across the room to greet them, her head high, rich auburn hair gleaming in the room's soft light.

"Good evening, Dr. Cassidy." Kathleen Kirk's voice was deep and cultured, and held a note of real welcoming warmth that was reassuring. "I'm so pleased you were free to join us this evening."

"Thank you for inviting me," Helen replied softly, studying the older woman as she placed her hand in the one outstretched to her. Although she was tall, she was delicately formed and the fine skin covering her face still held a faint, youthful glow despite the fine lines around her dark blue eyes.

During the brief exchange two men had come to stand behind Mrs. Kirk, and as she released Helen's hand she stepped to the side, said pleasantly, "My husband, George," nodding to a sandy-haired, distinguished-looking man not much taller than herself.

Helen took his hand, searching in vain for a resemblance to Marsh, as she murmured, "Mr. Kirk." Then she turned her head and caught her breath at Mrs. Kirk's, "And my father, Cullen Hannlon."

The resemblance here was uncanny. Helen knew that Marsh's grandfather had to be in his mid-seventies, yet nothing about him betrayed that fact. As tall as Marsh, his shoulders almost as broad, Cullen Hannlon stood straight, his large frame unbowed by time. He fit Marsh's name for him perfectly, for he was truly a bear of a man. The light blue eyes that held hers were the exact shade of his grandson's and they glowed with the same intent sharpness, and Helen would have bet her eyeteeth that his luxuriant shock of white hair had, in years past, been the same not-quite red as Marsh's.

Her hand was grasped, not taken, by his large, hardfingered, brown one, which reminded Helen of tough old leather. His entire appearance contrasted oddly with his deep, gentle voice.

"Well, Helen." No title from this quarter, Helen thought with amusement. "We finally meet. Of course," he teased, squeezing her hand. "Now that I see you I can understand why Marsh wanted to keep you to himself. You, my dear, are an extraordinarily beautiful woman."

Before Helen could find words to reply to this unbelievable old man, she heard Marsh laugh softly behind her and say sardonically, "You're wasting your time and breath, Cullen. Helen is immune to flattery."

Cullen favored Helen with a secret smile before turning suddenly fierce blue eyes on his grandson. "If you really believe that, son, you are a fool. And I know you are anything but that. No woman is immune to flattery, as indeed no man is; *if* it's the right kind of flattery."

Sauntering beside her as his mother ushered them into the room, Marsh's laughter deepened and he whispered close to her ear, "Imagine what he must have been like when he was young."

I don't have to imagine anything, Helen thought wryly. *All I have to do is turn my head and look at you.* The thought that Marsh would very likely be exactly the same as Cullen when he grew old was a strangely exciting one, and Helen quickly squashed it by thinking, *I won't be there to see it.* Forcing her mind away from the oddly bereft sensation her thoughts created, Helen turned her attention to what Mrs. Kirk was saying.

"You know my daughter, Kristeen, and her husband, Mike, of course."

Helen smiled at the young couple, seating herself on the delicately upholstered chair beside the matching settee they shared. "Hello, Kristeen, how are you? Mr. Darren. And how is your daughter?"

"She's perfect, Doctor, thank you." Kristeen smiled shyly. "And I feel wonderful. I wouldn't dare feel any other way after the amount of fussing this family of mine has done over me."

"Fussing, hell!" Cullen snorted impatiently. "This family has lost one woman through childbirth. I don't want to live through that again, so behave yourself, young woman, and let us care for you."

Although a smile played at her soft mouth, Kristeen answered demurely, "Yes, Grandfather."

"Father, please," Kathleen murmured softly, silencingly.

On his first statement Helen's eyes, full of questions, had swung to Cullen's, and now, although he grasped his daughter's shoulder gently, he answered the question. "I lost my wife three weeks after Kathleen was born." His voice was steady, yet Helen could sense the wealth of sorrow he still felt from his loss. "Megan had had a hard delivery and she was very weak. I was just getting started in the construction business and couldn't afford a full-time nurse."

His eyes darkened with pain, and Helen said urgently, "Mr. Hannlon, please don't. This isn't necessary." Her eyes flew to Marsh with a silent plea for help, but he didn't see her. His eyes were fastened on his grandfather, and incredibly Cullen's pain was reflected in them.

"She was so delighted with our daughter, she found pleasure in caring for her, even though it drained the little strength she had." He went on in that same quiet tone. "She was eighteen, I was twenty-one. Twenty-one," he repeated softly, then his eyes sharpened on Helen's. "Do you have any idea, I wonder, what losing his soulmate can do to a man?"

Helen felt trapped, pinned by those intense blue eyes, and she had the unreal, weird sensation that he was trying to tell her something important. Mentally shrugging off the feeling as compassion for his still obviously deep grief, Helen searched for suitable words.

"I—I don't know, sir. I've never lost a patient or had

to bring that kind of news to a husband. I can't even imagine—"

Marsh's soft voice saved Helen from floundering further, but in so doing he confused her even more, for there was a definite warning in his tone.

"Enough said, Cullen."

The old man's eyes shot a challenge at his grandson, one Marsh's very stance conveyed he was ready to meet. For several seconds the room seemed electrically charged and Helen could see her own confusion mirrored on the faces of the others as matching pairs of blue eyes silently dueled. Mr. Kirk relieved the tension with a dry gibe, addressed to Helen, but aimed at his son.

"May I get you an aperitif, Helen? You may need some alcoholic fortitude, as your escort seems to be spoiling for an argument."

"I'll get it." Marsh shot a grin at his father and a broad wink at his grandfather. "But let me assure you, she does not need it. I've tried arguing with Helen. I invariably lose."

"Good for Helen." Kathleen Kirk's smile stole the sting from her barb. "You are much too sure of yourself."

Later Helen was to wonder why she had hesitated over Marsh's parents' invitation. She had a delightful time. Kristeen and Mike were a lively couple, full of interesting and funny stories of times spent with their wide assortment of friends. Marsh periodically dropped dry, witty comments into their narrative as they shared some of their friends. Helen was surprised to find that Mr. and Mrs. Kirk were very well acquainted with several of her friends and colleagues, and that paved the way for further easy conversation.

But for Helen the most enjoyable part of the evening came from watching, in fascinated amusement, the thrust and parry between Cullen Hannlon and George Kirk. The play swung back and forth, George Kirk's wry, caustic lunges effortlessly deflected by Cullen's dry, acerbic ripostes. Helen had never witnessed anything quite like it before in her life.

Glancing at Marsh, Helen saw her own amusement mirrored in his eyes. That he got a kick out of watching the two men was obvious. Equally obvious was the deep love and respect he had for them. Knowing this warmed her, but for the life of her she couldn't figure out why. Why should it matter to her one way or the other, she asked herself, if he was capable of feeling abiding love, loyalty, respect?

When he took her home, Marsh kept to his promise not to pressure her. With a murmured, "I'll call you," he kissed her gently and left her staring after him in uncertain amazement.

It was toward the end of the following week that Helen first felt an uncomfortable twinge about Marsh's behavior. The fact that she couldn't exactly pinpoint what it was about his attitude made her uneasy. He was considerate and attentive, without actually dancing attendance on her, and yet there was something. It nagged her, but she couldn't quite put her finger on why.

January slipped into February and their relationship seemed at an impasse. Helen was seeing Marsh on an average of four nights a week, and surprisingly he did not call her on the nights she didn't see him. More surprising still was that he was adhering completely to his no-pressure promise. Was he losing interest? It was a question Helen asked herself more and more frequently as the days went by.

On the surface Marsh seemed as determined as before, at times more so. On the evening of Valentine's Day Kristeen and Mike were having a small get-together of friends, the first since their baby's birth, and they had asked Helen and Marsh to join them.

"I don't think so," Helen hedged when Marsh relayed Kris's invitation.

"Why not?" he asked, surprised. "I thought you liked Kris and Mike."

"I do," Helen replied promptly, then hesitated. She couldn't very well tell him she thought it unadvisable to get too involved with his family and friends, so she offered, lamely, "But it will be young married couples, won't it? I just don't think I'd fit in."

"Not fit in?" he exclaimed. "Helen, that's ridiculous. Of course you'd fit in. It will do you good to be around young women who are not your patients. Besides which" —he grinned—"I already told them we'd come."

He takes too much on himself, Helen fumed in frustration. *I really ought to put him back in his place.* She didn't at once, and then the moment was gone as he went on blandly to tell her who would be there. Not a large group, he informed her. Just a few close friends he shared with Kris and Mike.

On the fourteenth Marsh arrived at the apartment with a large elaborately decorated heart-shaped box of chocolates and a card, almost as large, that was covered with cupids and flowers and gushy sentiment. Reading the card, Helen frowned, unable to believe he really went in for that sort of mush, then, glancing up, she smiled ruefully at the devil gleam in his eye.

"There are times I'm convinced you are really quite mad, Marsh," she said, her tone deliberately crushing. It didn't work. He laughed at her, taunted, "I am quite mad. For you. I couldn't resist the urge to watch your face as you read it." He paused, then chided, nodding at the candy, "Aren't you going to offer me a piece?"

"You're impossible," Helen murmured, tugging at the end of the large bow on the ribbon that surrounded the box. Glancing up to smile at him, she felt her heartbeats quicken, her mouth go dry. The gleam had disappeared and there was a waiting stillness about him that warned her. Lifting the heart-shaped lid carefully, she bit her lip, then sat down slowly. At the *V* of the heart several pieces of the candy had been removed and in their place was nestled a small jeweler's box.

For a moment, thinking the box contained a ring, pure panic gripped her. Then reason reasserted itself as she realized the box was larger, flatter than a ring box. With trembling fingers she removed the box, lifted the lid, a small gasp whispering through her lips. In the glow from the lamp beside her chair the gold inside the box seemed to glitter and wink at her. Very carefully she extracted the intricately worked and, at the price of gold, obviously expensive chains, one for the neck and a smaller one for the wrist.

Handling the delicate pieces gently, Helen looked up at the silently waiting man in front of her, her eyes unknowingly telegraphing her words.

"Marsh, they're beautiful, but I—"

"Don't say it, Helen," Marsh warned softly. He lifted the candy box from her lap and slid it onto the end table. "Stand up and I'll fasten them on for you."

Standing on legs that felt none too steady, Helen watched as he clasped the small chain on her wrist. The chain was loose and slid partway down the back of her hand.

"I didn't realize your wrist was so slender," he said softly. "Should I have it made smaller for you?"

A sudden, unreasonable feeling of possessiveness gripped her, and not even knowing why, she didn't want to remove the chain. "No!" Too hasty, she chided herself, tempering it with a small laugh. "I think I like it loose like that."

"Yes," Marsh murmured, studying the effect of the gold against her skin. "Something sexy about it." His eyes lifted to hers and what they told her sent her pulses racing.

Without waiting to see if she'd reply, he moved around her to fasten the neck chain. He brushed her hair to one

The Game Is Played

side, and Helen felt a chill at the touch of his fingers on the sensitive skin at the back of her neck. The chain was fastened, then his hands encircled her throat.

"They look like fine slave chains," he breathed softly. "Do they make you my slave, Helen?"

The chill turned into a strong shiver that zigzagged the length of her spine, down the back of her legs.

"Marsh . . . oh, Marsh, stop."

It was a strangled protest against his mouth, moving along the side of her neck; his hands, moving down the silky material of her blouse, over the firm mounds of her breasts.

"How long are you going to hold out, Helen?" his breath whispered against her skin. Then she was turned around into his arms, his hands holding her tightly to the hard length of his body. "How long should the slave be allowed to torture her master?" His hands fastened on her hips, drawing her still closer, making her all too aware of his meaning.

Helen gasped at the word "master," but her retort was lost inside his mouth. His kiss was a hungry, urgent demand, and Helen's hands, which had grasped his wrists to pull his hands away from her hips, slid up his arms to his shoulders and clung. He hadn't kissed her like this in weeks, and until that moment Helen hadn't fully realized how much she'd wanted him to. The realization was a sobering one. Giving a firm push against his shoulders, she stepped back away from him.

"Marsh, stop it," she cried shakily. "If you think my accepting these gives you the right to—" She paused, fingers fumbling at the clasp on the wrist chain. "You can take it back."

"Leave it," Marsh snapped, his large hand covering her fingers, stilling their trembling. "There are no strings on it, or anything else I may give you. Not even on myself." He drew a harsh breath, then added more softly, "You know what I want, Helen. I made my feelings clear at the beginning. But you can set the rules, you make the conditions. Only, for God's sake, do it soon. Don't let me hang indefinitely."

Helen felt shaken and confused. Oh, yes, she thought wildly, she knew what he wanted. He wanted a bed partner, the triumph of subduing the cool, *older* lady doctor. Were there rules and conditions to that kind of relationship? If there were, Helen was positive that, for all his assurances to the contrary, he fully intended to set them.

He waited several minutes, and when she didn't speak or respond in anyway, he spun away, walked to the closet, yanked her coat from the hanger, and snapped, "Let's get out of here. Kris and Mike are probably wondering where we are."

Still without speaking, Helen slipped into the coat, buttoned up with a calmness she was far from feeling inside. He was angry. Really angry. His eyes held a chilling coldness he'd never turned on her before. His control seemed to crack when she returned his stare with a forced coolness of her own.

"You're enjoying every minute of this, aren't you?" he ground through clenched teeth.

"I don't know what you mean."

"Of course not," he taunted silkily. "Have your fun while you can, love, because your line's about played out."

Marsh maintained a cool, withdrawn silence during the entire twenty-five-minute drive to his sister's home. Helen's nerves, already frayed when they left the apartment, stretched and grew more taut as each silent second followed another. She was twisting the narrow chain around her wrist, on the verge of telling him to turn the car around and take her home, when he pulled up and parked along the curb in front of a row of fairly new, modern town houses. There were other cars parked along the curb and two, bumper to bumper, in the narrow driveway that led to a garage adjacent to the house.

When Marsh walked through the doorway of his sister's house, he left outside the cold, angry man he'd been for over a half hour. A slight widening of her eyes was her only outward reaction to his sudden change, but he saw it and shook his head once sharply at her before turning a smiling face to the people gathered inside the long living room.

Besides Kris and Mike there were four other couples in the room. Names were tossed at her casually, with an aside from Marsh not to worry, he'd sort them out for her later, but although the surnames were lost, she caught and held on to the first names. There were Bob and Donna, and Charles and Irene, all the same age as Kris and Mike. Then there were Ray and Betty, and Grant and Mary Ellen, a few years older than the others, more Marsh's age.

There were no awkward moments. The introductions dispensed with, Helen was drawn into the conversation so effortlessly, it had her wondering if the whole thing had been rehearsed. She would reject the idea a short time later.

Before many minutes had passed, Helen reached the conclusion that the affection these people obviously held for each other was a holdover from childhood. They accepted her without question because she was with Marsh, it was as simple as that.

Marsh slipped into a chair and the conversation with an easy camaraderie. Letting the conversation swirl around her, Helen observed him, as she had the evening she'd been at his parents' home. All traces of his earlier tension and anger were gone. He laughed often, a delightful sound that drew a reciprocal response from the others. It soon became evident to Helen as she watched him that, although he genuinely liked all of the guests, there was a special bond between him and Grant.

Their banter back and forth, as they argued over a recent Philadelphia 76ers game, was much the same as Marsh indulged in with Moe. Listening more to the tone of their voices rather than their words, Helen glanced up in surprise when Grant asked, "Don't you agree, Helen?"

"I'm sorry." Helen smiled apologetically. "I'm afraid I wasn't listening."

"Grant said that it looks like the 76ers may have a winning year." Marsh's tone held a faint trace of annoyance. "He asked if you agree with him."

"I have no idea." Helen met Marsh's cool glance with equal coolness before turning to Grant with a warm smile. "I don't follow basketball at all." A teasing note covered her serious tone. "Does that make me a traitor to my city?"

"If it does, you have plenty of company," Mary Ellen answered for her husband.

"I thought you liked basketball." Grant's pleasant, ordinary face held an injured look that matched his tone.

"I do." Mary Ellen laughed. "I also like watching the Eagles play football, the Flyers play hockey, and the Phillies play baseball, but not necessarily as a steady diet."

Grant turned to Marsh with eyebrows raised exaggeratedly high. "Do you get the feeling our conversation has been boring the ladies?"

"The thought has occurred," Marsh replied dryly. "Perhaps we should hit the ball into their court and let them choose a topic."

It was all the encouragement Mary Ellen needed. Eyes bright with amusement, she launched into a hilarious account of a comedy-of-errors skiing trip she and Grant had taken the previous year.

During the course of the evening Helen learned, from Mary Ellen, that her assumption about the closeness between Marsh and Grant was correct. They had been friends from grade school, were in fact closer than most brothers. Marsh had been best man at their wedding and was their son's godfather. A sudden stifled, closed-in sensation feathered over Helen when Mary Ellen finished, "Both Grant and I unashamedly adore Marsh and would love to see him content and happy with a family of his own." Her eyes sought the man in question, a gentle smile curved her lips as she studied him. "Marsh will be thirty-one next month," she said softly. "And though he claims to be having a ball in his bachelor existence, everyone who loves him knows it's a lie. He's a steady, roots-deep-in-the-ground sort of man; he's ready to settle down." Her eyes swung to Helen's face, her smile deepened. "The problem *has* been finding the right woman."

Unease joined the stifled sensations rippling along Helen's nerves, and changing the subject quickly, she figuratively backed away from Mary Ellen's none too subtle revelations.

Midway through the evening Kris announced that a light supper had been set out on the dining room table. After serving herself sparingly from the wide assortment of food, Helen followed Marsh back to the living room and allowed him to draw her down onto a large pouf beside his chair.

"What do you think of Grant?" His bland tone didn't deceive her for a second. She could actually feel the intentness with which he awaited her answer.

"I like him." She answered with frank honesty. "And I think the easygoing manner he shows to the world is a facade that disguises a very determined man." She glanced up at him, smiled slightly. "I think he could give a woman a very bad time, if he was so inclined."

"Couldn't we all?" Marsh slanted her a wicked glance and laughed softly. "But I'm inclined to think that Mary Ellen could probably give him a damned good run for his money, if *she* was so inclined." His grin was every bit as wicked as his glance. "You want to try *me* on?"

Ignoring the lightning shaft of excitement that zigzagged through her, Helen returned his stare thoughtfully, then replied coolly, "You'd lose, you know."

His soft laughter was a gentle assault on her senses. "Not on your stethoscope, sweetheart."

Even though his tone had been teasing, Helen felt a chill of warning replace the excitement deep inside. She had no time to analyze the feeling however as he went on quietly. "I've invited Grant and Mary Ellen to join us for dinner at my apartment Saturday night." He arched an inquiring eyebrow at her. "All right?"

"Yes, of course," Helen replied. "But right now I think I'd better go home. I have a full schedule tomorrow."

After the usual time-consuming flurry of leave-taking and when they were finally in the car, Helen asked curiously, "Were you planning to cook dinner yourself?"

"And poison some of my best friends?" Marsh asked seriously. "No, love, I'll let Moe do the honors this time. Unless"—he shot her a teasing glance—"you'd like to do it."

For one insane moment Helen was actually tempted, then common sense reasserted itself. "I'll pass, thank you." As he stopped at a stop sign at that moment, she turned to look at him directly, her eyes cool. "I'm not in the least domestic." Another card, unplanned, was placed onto the invisible table between them.

Marsh played a trump. "It doesn't matter, I can always *hire* domestic help."

They both knew they were no longer talking about the upcoming dinner, and thinking it judicious to play her cards more carefully in future, Helen remained silent. Could he, she wondered, be aware that she'd dealt herself a hand in this game he was playing? The thought nagged at her for some minutes, then she dismissed it as ridiculous. He was far too sure of himself to ever consider the possibility.

Helen was late arriving for dinner. Marsh had said they'd eat at seven thirty but, as Grant and Mary Ellen were coming at seven for predinner drinks, he'd pick her up at six thirty.

Just before five Helen received an emergency call from

the hospital. A self-induced abortion case had been brought in, she was informed. A young girl, still in her teens. As the girl's mother, frantic with worry, was a patient of Helen's, she had insisted, hysterically, that Helen be called.

Helen recognized the woman's name immediately and said she'd be there as soon as possible. She left the apartment without a thought to Marsh's dinner, her mind on the possible physical damage to the girl, and the mental damage to the mother.

The woman had come to Helen with a minor problem the same week she'd opened her office and returned for twice-yearly checkups ever since. Honest, hardworking and unassuming, she had made a career of taking care of her husband, raising her family. Helen knew what the young girl's action could do to the woman. So much for the joys and rewards of family life, Helen thought cynically as she drove to the hospital.

It was not until she had parked her car, illegally, in the emergency entrance and was striding toward the wide glass doors, that she remembered Marsh.

Stopping at the nurses station, Helen asked where the girl was, if someone could take care of her car, and would the nurse make a phone call for her. In that order. The nurse, a middle-aged veteran, echoed Helen's brisk tone. The girl was being prepped for O.R.; she could rest easy about her car; and, certainly, the phone call would be made.

Helen asked for a piece of paper, on which she scribbled Marsh's name and phone number, then she told the nurse tersely, "Just tell him there's been an emergency and I'll get there as soon as I can. And thank you."

The nurse's quiet "You're welcome, Doctor" floated on the empty air where Helen had stood. Moving at a fast clip toward the elevators, Helen glanced at the large wall clock. It was twenty-three minutes since she'd received the call.

It was messy and touch and go, and the hands on the O.R. wall clock moved inexorably from number to number, but Helen saved the young girl's life.

Exhausted, filled with rage and bitter frustration at the idea that in an age of almost instant legal abortion on demand, a young girl, terrified at the results of her own foolishness, would inflict such damage on herself rather than go to her parents, Helen cleaned up and went to the lounge where those parents waited.

On entering the room, Helen's eyes went first to the girl's father. Of medium height, stockily built, the man held his face in such rigid control, it looked as if it were carved in stone. Shifting her gaze, Helen's eyes met the anxious, tear-drenched eyes of his wife. Lips quivering, the woman whispered, "Doctor?"

"She'll live," Helen stated bluntly, steeling herself against the fresh tears that ran down the woman's pale cheeks.

"Thank God." The low, choked-out prayer came from the husband. "May we see her?"

Helen's eyes swung back to his, now suspiciously bright with moisture. "She'll be in recovery for a while." Compassion tugged at her heart, softened her tone. "You both look on the verge of collapse. Why don't you take your wife down to the lunchroom, have some coffee and something to eat." She underlined the last three words heavily.

"Was there much damage, Doctor?" The woman had gained control of herself. Her eyes were clear, steady.

"Some," Helen sighed. "But she is alive and will recover. We'll discuss the damage, both physical and mental, later. Right now I prescribe a strong shot of caffeine for both of you." She was rewarded with a weak smile. "The nurse at the floor station will tell you when you can see her. If you can arrange to be in the hospital tomorrow morning when I make my rounds, we'll talk after I've examined your daughter."

"We'll be here." The man beat his wife into speech.

After again advising them to have something to eat, Helen left the room and went to collect her coat and bag, not even bothering to repair her makeup.

Marsh opened the door seconds after Helen touched the bell and, after a quick glance at her face, murmured, "Was it bad?"

"Yes," she answered simply as she entered the apartment's tiny foyer.

Standing behind her, holding her coat as she slipped out of it, he asked, "A hard delivery?"

"No." Helen turned to face him, waited until he'd hung up her coat and turned around again before adding, "A young girl tried to commit suicide the hard way."

"Abortion?" Incredulity laced his tone.

"Yes."

His eyes, tinged with concern, searched her face. "Is she all right?"

"She's alive," Helen sighed wearily. "Oh, Marsh, it was grim." Without hesitation, without even thinking, she walked right into him, rested her forehead against his chest.

For a split second he was still, then his arms came around her, tightened protectively. "It's all right, love," he murmured against her hair. "You're home."

Too tired, for the moment, to think, she barely heard his words, let alone the meaning behind them. His hand moved and tugged at her hair to turn her face up to his. In fascination Helen watched his firm mouth lowering slowly to hers, lost to the presence of the two people sitting in the living room unashamedly watching the tableau with interest.

Marsh's mouth was tender, gentle with hers. As the kiss lengthened, deepened, Helen felt the tensions and frustrations of the last hours drain out of her. Sighing deeply, she returned his kiss fervently. Her hands were moving up his chest to his neck when he suddenly stepped back, a rueful smile curving his lips.

"We have guests, love," he said softly. "Come have a drink and relax a little before dinner."

Marsh turned her toward the living room, his arm, angled from shoulder to waist across her back, holding her close to his side. Helen felt the warmth of embarrassment mount her cheeks on encountering the expressions of concern for her, written clearly on the faces of Grant and Mary Ellen.

"Come sit by me, Helen, while Marsh gets your drink," Mary Ellen invited warmly. "You look completely shattered."

With a tired smile Helen sank onto the sofa beside Mary Ellen, accepted the glass of wine Marsh handed her, took a small sip, smiled her appreciation and thanks to him, then turned her attention to what Mary Ellen was saying.

"We couldn't help but overhear what you said when you came in. What a horrible thing to do."

"Yes," Helen agreed. "It was pretty horrible for her parents too. I am of the opinion that raising children can be heartbreaking at times."

"But rewarding as well," Mary Ellen assured firmly. "Grant and I have had a few bad moments with our two boys, but I wouldn't give them up for the world." She turned her serious gaze onto her husband. "Would you, Grant?"

"No," Grant answered simply. "I think that by the time they are fully grown the good times will have, by far, outweighed the bad."

"I think on that profound note, we'll go have dinner," Marsh said, quietly reaching for Helen's hand.

Conversation was easy and relaxed while they ate Moe's expertly prepared veal scallopini.

"Do you ski, Helen?" Mary Ellen asked suddenly, paus-

The Game Is Played

ing in the act of spooning up the rich dessert Moe had concocted.

"Yes," Helen admitted, adding, "not expertly, but well enough to handle the smaller slopes."

"And I know Marsh is very good." Mary Ellen's eyes lit with an idea. "Grant and I, along with several other couples, are going up to the Poconos next Thursday for a long weekend of skiing. Why don't you two join us?"

"I don't think—" That was as far as Helen got with her refusal, for Marsh quietly interrupted her.

"Sounds good to me." He lifted an eyebrow at her. "What do you say, Helen? Do you think you could get someone to fill in for you? You could stand a break, especially after today."

"Well, I suppose I could, but—"

"The hospital won't fall apart in four days, Helen," Marsh urged.

"Well—" Helen hesitated, then gave in. "Let me see if I can arrange something."

Leaving the table, Helen went to the phone in the living room, dialed, then spoke quietly a few moments. When she turned back to the others, she was smiling.

"All set." Helen's eyes sought, then found the blue ones. "Dr. Munziack will be on call for me. He owes me one." Her smile deepened. "As a matter of fact he owes me several. I can be ready to leave as soon as I've made my rounds Thursday morning."

The remainder of the evening was spent in making plans and generally getting to know each other. Marsh went to the stereo and placed a record on the machine, then waited for the music to begin to adjust the volume. Helen glanced up in surprise on hearing the opening strains of Tchaikovsky's *Fifth Symphony*. Marsh grinned at her, shrugged.

"What can I tell you?" His grin widened. "I'm a Tchaikovsky nut."

Helen managed to keep a straight face, but her amusement came through in her tone. "And all this time I thought it was a ploy you used when—ah—entertaining."

Laughing softly, he strolled across the room to her, placed a hand on her shoulder, and gave her a punishing squeeze, blandly ignoring the confused glances Grant and Mary Ellen exchanged.

It was not until later that night when Helen lay on her bed, tired yet sleepless, that the closed-in feeling returned. Only now it was so much stronger, so cloying, Helen sat up quickly, breathing deeply. Marsh was drawing her slowly, but inexorably, into his life. His words of earlier that night crept into her mind. "It's all right, love. You're home."

She slid down onto the pillows again, her mind worrying at his words. Calmer now, her thinking process coolly detached, Helen reached the conclusion that Marsh had decided to pull out all stops. He had every intention of winning this particular game. *And you,* she told herself dismally, *are playing right into his hands.* Her last coherent thought as she drifted into sleep was that the last thing she should be considering now was a long weekend in the mountains with him.

ments after she'd replaced it. Without halfway trying, she could imagine Marsh's reaction in the morning when her service informed him that Dr. Cassidy was out of town and no, they didn't know where she'd gone.

The flight, late that night, was quiet and uneventful, and although she didn't think she'd be able to, Helen slept through most of it. Her father, tall, slim, was waiting for her, a smile of eager expectancy on his sun-weathered face.

With a feeling of coming home, being safe, Helen walked into his outstretched arms, closed her eyes against the sudden hot sting of tears.

"What's this?" Robert Cassidy felt the shiver that rippled through his daughter's slim frame, and grasping her shoulders, he held her away from him, studied her face carefully. Noting the brightness of her eyes, his brows rose slowly.

"A man, Helen?"

Helen didn't even consider pretense. He was the one person she could never fool with her cool exterior. In fact there were times while Helen was growing up that he seemed to know what she was going to do before she did. And now, her feelings raw and she more vulnerable than she'd ever been before in her life, she didn't even try.

"Yes."

That one softly murmured word spoke volumes to him, and his eyes sharpened while his tone softened.

"Want to talk about it?"

"No." Helen gave a quick shake of her head, then smiled ruefully. "At least not tonight." She paused before adding, "I have to think it through for myself first, Dad. Right now I'm uncertain as to how to handle this and I don't like the feeling, it's not me."

"That's for sure." One arm draped over her shoulders, Robert paced his long stride to hers as they went to pick up her suitcase. In tune mentally, as they had always been, they dropped the subject, Robert knowing that when she was ready Helen would tell him, if not everything, enough to put him in the picture.

Her mother was waiting at the door of the small ranch-style home her parents had bought on the outskirts of Phoenix, her still-lovely face mirroring her happiness at seeing her firstborn. For the second time in less than an hour Helen was enfolded within loving arms and again felt the quick rush of tears.

No less shrewd than her husband Laura Cassidy was quick to notice the change in her daughter.

"Darling, what's wrong?" she asked anxiously. "Are you ill?"

The words, so similar to the ones Marsh had said to her just a few hours ago, brought a fresh surge of moisture. What was wrong with her anyway? Helen thought irritably. She hadn't been this quick to tears during adolescence. With a determined effort she controlled her features, steadied her voice.

"No, Mother, I'm not ill," she answered firmly. "The last couple of weeks have been hectic, I'm very tired. Nothing more serious than that."

"Well, that's a relief," Laura sighed deeply, her sentiments reflected on her face. "Come sit down. I have a pot of herb tea ready for you, and as soon as you've had a cup it's bed for you."

Helen's laughter was a warm, natural reaction to her mother's dictate. Not since her fifteenth year had she heard that note of firmness in her mother's voice.

"Oh, Mother." Helen bestowed a brief hug on her parent. "It's so good to see you."

Surrounded by parental love, cocooned within the silence of her father's tacit patience, Helen slept deeply and refreshingly, undisturbed by uneasy thoughts of a handsome young man bent on possession.

Rob's welcome was no less enthusiastic than their parents' had been, as was his pretty, somewhat flighty wife and their two fresh-faced boys. But as their mother and father had done the previous evening, he saw at once that all was not well with her.

"What's the problem, big sister?" Rob asked bluntly the first time they were alone for a minute.

"Mind your own business, Sonny," Helen quipped gently, returning the grin he threw her at her deliberate use of his childhood nickname.

"The subject not open for discussion, Helen?"

"Not just yet, Rob," she answered softly. They were standing together at the barbecue grill at the end of the large patio outside the kitchen of Rob's much larger ranch-style home a few miles from her parents'. In between brushing globs of sauce on the chicken sizzling on the grill, Rob slanted her a sharp-eyed glance.

"Will you answer one question?" He turned to face her fully, his gaze level.

"Depends on the question," Helen hedged.

"Daddy." The voice of Rob's eldest filtered through the kitchen screen door.

"In a minute, Chuck," Rob tossed over his shoulder, his eyes locked on hers. Then, his tone lower, he asked, "Is there a man involved?"

"Yes, but that's all I'm saying."

"Daddy, Mommy said you should come in for the salad things." Chuck's young voice was a shade louder.

"Paint your chicken, Sonny," Helen gibed, grinning as she turned toward the house. "I'll help Chuck with the salad."

Rob's hand caught her arm, held her still a moment. "If you need me, want someone to tell your troubles to, I'm here, big sister."

Something lodged, painfully, in Helen's throat at his gentle tone. Her slim hand covered his, tightened briefly in thanks. Turning quickly, she hurried toward the house, a tiny break in her voice as she called, "Daddy's busy, Chuck. I'll help you."

In the general confusion of fixing a salad with Chuck, fussing over her youngest nephew, Mike, when he woke from his nap, and receiving a rundown from her sister-in-law of both boys' activities since she'd last seen them, Helen was able to bring her shaky emotions under control.

The week passed pleasantly and much too fast. As her tension eased and her usual confidence reasserted itself, Helen lost the urge to confide in her family.

In the afternoon of the day before Helen's scheduled return to Philly, she had a few minutes alone with her father in the tiny room everyone teasingly referred to as "Dad's study." Feeling she owed her father some sort of an explanation, yet not sure how to begin, Helen sighed with relief when her father ended the short uncomfortable silence.

"Feeling better, Helen?"

"Yes, Dad, I—" Helen hesitated, searching for words. His astuteness made it unnecessary.

"You look better too." Robert studied her carefully, warmly. "If you don't want to talk about it, Helen, then don't. But just remember, I'm here for you if you need me."

Not for the first time, Helen gave a silent thanks for the family she'd been blessed with. Her mother had fussed over her all week, coaxing her to eat, to rest, but though her eyes mirrored her concern, she had not questioned her once. And now her father's words had echoed Rob's. "If you need me, I'm here." They would not pry or in any way presume to infringe on her privacy, but quietly, lovingly, they let her know they were there for her. It helped.

"Thanks, Dad." Helen smiled her gratitude. "I'd really rather not talk about it. Right now I'm feeling a little unsure of myself with this man, who, if you don't mind, will remain nameless." Robert nodded his head briefly. "Please don't worry and don't let Mother and Rob worry either." Her voice firmed with determination. "I'll resolve it."

"Of course you will." Robert's tone was equally firm. "We all need breathing space at times, Helen, when things seem to crowd in, threaten to overwhelm us. You have a good head on your shoulders. I doubt there's little you can't handle."

But then, Helen thought wryly, *you don't know Marshall Kirk.*

Her flight home was every bit as uneventful as the one west had been. She boarded the plane feeling more relaxed than she had in weeks, but tension began building as the big jet drew ever nearer to the East Coast.

There was Marsh's justifiable anger to be faced. What had been his reaction to her disappearance? Perhaps, after his initial irritation cooled, he had put her from his mind and gone about the business of finding a more accommodating companion. The mere thought of him with another woman brought a mixture of pain and self-derision. *Do you know,* she asked herself bitingly, *what exactly you do want?* Flipping open the magazine her father had bought for her, she flipped through the pages, not yet ready to face a truthful answer to her own question.

It was early evening when Helen entered her apartment. After depositing her suitcase in the bedroom, she went into the kitchen, made herself a cup of tea, then called her service for messages left while she was gone. The crisp voice at the other end of the line rattled on for several minutes and ended with, "And a Mr. Kirk has called twice a day, morning and evening, every day. He was very put-out the first morning, insisted I tell him where you were. I had some difficulty convincing him I had no idea where you'd gone."

"Yes . . . well, I'll take care of it," Helen said softly. "Thank you."

Her finger pressed the disconnect button, then moved

to press Marsh's number. While his phone rang, she drew a deep breath, steeling herself for his anger.

"Hello." The voice was so harsh, so ragged sounding, Helen was not sure it was he.

"Marsh?"

There was silence for a full ten seconds before Helen heard his breath being expelled very slowly.

"Where were you?" His very softness threw her off balance, robbed her of speech. "Helen, I've been damned near out of my mind. Where were you?" The tone was rough now, demanding an answer.

"With my family." Helen found her voice, even managed to keep it steady. "In Arizona. I was tired, Marsh, and I just couldn't face that skiing trip. I'm sorry but—"

"Who cares about the stupid skiing trip?" he cut in roughly. "Are you all right?"

"Yes, of course, but—"

"No buts," Marsh again cut in. "If you had to get away for a while, then you did. I told you no strings, Helen, I meant it." His voice went low, held a hint of amusement. "I've got you running scared, don't I?"

"Scared?" she scoffed, a little shakily. "Of you? You flatter yourself."

His soft laughter hummed along the wire to tickle her ear, tinge her cheeks pink. "Do I? I don't think so," he drawled. "Why don't you give up? You're going to lose, Helen."

"I don't know what you mean," she snapped. "I must hang up now, I have some more calls to make."

"Okay, coward." Helen shivered as he laughed again. "One more thing and I'll let you go." His tone softened. "Do you feel rested now?"

Suspicious of his tone but not sure why, Helen hesitated a second before admitting, "Yes."

"Good, then you'll be up to having dinner with Cullen tomorrow night." Before she could object, refuse, he whispered, "Good night, love," and hung up.

THE GAME IS PLAYED

Cullen was the perfect host, charming and amusing. Helen knew, for she had seen at unguarded moments that everyone was speculating about the seriousness of her and Marsh's relationship. Everyone, that was, except Cullen. In the relatively short amount of time they were with him, she was left in little doubt that the "old bear" was no longer speculating. He had reached the conclusion that the young "cub" had found a mate. He made no attempt to hide the fact that his conclusion pleased him.

Helen did not like deceiving anyone. But most especially she did not like deceiving Cullen. If he was an "old bear," he was an extremely gentle one, at least with her. After that evening the game became not only nerve-racking but distasteful, and Helen told herself repeatedly to end it.

Curiosity kept her from following the dictates of her own common sense. How long, she wondered, would Marsh drag out the farce? As the weeks slipped by, Helen became certain that the game was losing its appeal for him, for he made no overt moves toward her. Since the night he gave her the gold chains and his promise of no pressure, he had not been in her apartment. When he brought her home, it was to the door, where, with a light, passionless kiss and a casual good night, he left her.

But still he made no indication that he was ready to either abandon or end the game, even though the challenge she had represented had apparently lost its allure. Helen, barely able to face her own accusing eyes in the mirror, doggedly followed his lead.

What did she think she was doing? The question repeated itself with monotonous regularity. He was becoming a habit, a habit, moveover, that was growing stronger with each passing day. Being with him was torment, being away from him was agony. She wanted him desperately and the intensity of that growing desperation confused and frightened her. At times she lost sight of what the game was all about and longed for the feel of his arms around her, his hard body pressed to hers. She had no basis of comparison for her feelings except the time she had spent with Carl, and even in that, the comparison was minute. At no time, either while they were dating or after they had become engaged, had her feelings for Carl ever made her lose sight of her goal. And so she worried. Worried about her own increasing need to be with him. Worried about the thoughts that tormented her late in the night, driving her out of her bed to pace the floor restlessly. Worried about the end that had to come soon if she was to retain a shred of her self-respect.

Marsh seemed in no way concerned with similar worries. And seemingly without being aware he was doing it, he was wearing down her resistance. He took it for granted that she would spend most of her free time with him and had taken to calling her at the office to inform her of the plans he'd made, the invitations he'd accepted for both of them.

Sundays they were together exclusively. Hour by hour, hand in hand, they walked. They explored Germantown, strolled on the cobblestone street by the brick houses in Elfreth's Alley, a one-block-long street near the riverfront that is one of the oldest streets in America. They spent hours in Independence Hall and the National Historical Park and seriously discussed the possibility of the first United States flag being made in the Betsy Ross House. Then they went back into Fairmont Park; this time Marsh succeeded in drawing her down to the river to watch the sculling crews working out. Sunday nights were the only nights Helen had no difficulty sleeping. With all the exercise and fresh air she was usually out cold within minutes after sliding between the sheets.

By mid-March Helen had a problem. On Saturday afternoon, after ushering her last patient out of her office, she sat staring at the square, white, gold-embossed invitation she held gingerly in one hand. A frown creasing her forehead, she read, then reread, the gold script. The invitation was for a retirement party the following Saturday to honor the much-respected and very well-liked head of OB-GYN. at the hospital. True, it gave very short notice of the affair, but as she knew the man's decision to retire had been on the spur of the moment because of health reasons, this was not why Helen frowned.

Her problem was Marsh. As the invitation had been issued to Helen and guest, she was, of course, at liberty to ask him to escort her. But that was the fly in her particular ointment. Thus far she had deliberately avoided introducing him to any of her small circle of friends. At regular intervals he had chided her about it, but she had dodged his sardonic barbs with the excuse that her friends, most with full family lives, were in an after-the-holidays entertaining slump. As it was now over two months since the holiday season, Helen knew there were large holes in the excuse and she had been searching her mind for a replacement.

Now, tucked in with the usual mundane Saturday mail, was an invitation she could not very well ignore. Helen's friends, knowing her as well as possible, had thought little of her absence—except that she might be overworking. They knew that she was a very private person, that she preferred a quiet evening of conversation or a really good concert, to overcrowded parties, whether in private homes or the organized ones in large hotels or country clubs. But they also knew of the true affection she had for her imminent chief and would be surprised if she bypassed his party.

Tapping the card with a neatly trimmed, unpainted fingernail, Helen wondered what to do. She knew Marsh. She also knew that if she told him that she could not see him next Saturday night he would torment her subtly until she told him why. She could lie, of course, but somehow the thought of lying outright to him was repulsive to her. When her phone buzzed, Helen tossed the card onto her desk with relief. Lifting the receiver, she pressed the blinking button and said briskly, "Dr. Cassidy."

Without preliminaries Marsh inquired, "Are you almost through there, Helen?"

"Yes, why?"

"No little mother about to increase the population? No meetings? No hairdresser apopintment or shopping to do?"

"No," Helen answered patiently. "Why, Marsh?"

"I'm stranded at a construction site and hoped I could coax you into picking me up." Marsh hesitated, then bribed. "I'll buy you lunch."

"What do you mean you're stranded? Where is your car?"

"I put it in the garage this morning for inspection," he explained. "It won't be ready until later this afternoon. As a matter of fact you could drop me at the garage after we've had lunch, okay?"

"Yes, of course I'll pick you up," Helen agreed at once. "But what construction site are you stranded at, and why?" Helen's puzzlement was obvious. "I mean—why are you at *any* construction site?"

"It's one of Cullen's babies." Marsh laughed. "There was a snarl up here, and as always, he called and told me to come straighten it out."

"And did you?" Helen asked dryly.

"Just about." He spoke with equal dryness. He gave her directions to the site, which was located some distance outside the city, then said, "When you get here, park the car and come into the trailer office." A hint of laughter touched his tone. "Just in case the unsnarler gets snarled."

As Helen prepared to leave the office her glance was caught by the white card on her desk. After a moment's hesitation she picked it up, slipped it back into its envelope, and stuffed it into the depths of her handbag.

The Game Is Played

Giving a mental shrug, she thought, *I'll decide about that later.*

She found the site without difficulty, and after parking the car, she made her way carefully over the uneven and still frozen ground, pausing to read the large white sign posted on the wooden fence that completely surrounded the site. The sign informed her that the construction under way would result in a high-rise apartment complex, that it had been designed by the architectural firm of Wanner, Freebold, and Wanner, and was being erected by the Hannlon Building and Construction Firm, Cullen Hannlon, President.

A small smile curved Helen's lips as she read the last, then her eyes perplexed, her gaze returned to the name Wanner.

"Learning anything?"

Helen jumped at the sound of the teasing voice close to her ear. Not bothering to answer his question, she murmured, "That name Wanner seems vaguely familiar."

"I'm not surprised." Marsh laughed softly. "You were introduced to it a few weeks ago." At her confused stare he nudged. "Grant? Mary Ellen?"

"Oh!" Helen's eyes cleared and she smiled, remembering. "Last names barely registered that night. I was relieved I could hold on to the first."

"Grant's the second Wanner," he offered. "The firm was started by his father and uncle. Grant joined it as a very junior member when he got out of school. He's really very good," he added. "As a matter of fact he designed this building."

While he was talking, Marsh led her to a small trailer some yards away and guided her up the steps and into what appeared to be a shambles. Watching her expression as her eyes circled the mess, Marsh laughed aloud.

"Don't be deceived, love. I assure you the construction boss knows exactly where everything is and can lay his hand on whatever he wants at a moment's notice." Strolling into the trailer's tiny kitchen area, he asked. "Would you like some coffee?"

Helen opened her mouth to say "Yes, please," but nothing came out. Lips forming a large *O* her eyes went wide at the loud sound of gears grinding, tires screeching, and then the scream of a man. Before she could close her mouth, blink her eyes, Marsh was by her and lunging out the door, the last part of his growled "Son of a—" lost to her. In half an instant she was spinning around, running after him, stumbling over the torn-up, slippery earth.

Dodging ice-skimmed puddles of water, Helen tried to make sense of the blurred scene that met her eyes. Men were running from all directions toward a large piece of machinery lying drunkenly on its side. As she reached the fringes of the crowded men Helen could hear Marsh's voice, sharp, clear, issuing orders tersely. One man detached himself from the group, ran toward another large machine.

From inside the circle of men Helen heard the agonized speech of a man, heard him groan, and her hand pushed against a rock-hard male arm.

"Let me through," she ordered as sharply as Marsh had. "I'm a doctor."

Moving aside respectfully, the man tapped the shoulder of the man in front of him, relaying Helen's order. Moving through the men, Helen took in the situation. When the machine had toppled over, it had trapped the driver and crushed his leg against the ground, and now half in, half out, of the thing, the man lay in a crumpled heap in the driver's seat. His lips were twisted in pain, his eyes were glazed, and his face was gray with shock.

Without a thought to the sheer nylon that gave no protection whatever to her knees, Helen dropped to the ground beside him, her fingers going to his wrist. Not liking what she felt, she ordered softly, "Marsh, you have got to move this monster off of him." Not for a minute doubting his ability to do so.

"We will," Marsh said just as softly. "An ambulance has been called. I've sent for blankets and—" A man walked up beside him, handed him a white box with a red cross on it. "And here's the first-aid box. There's a syringe of morphine inside."

Without questioning or even looking up, Helen held out her hand. A saturated piece of cotton was placed in her fingers, and after swabbing the man's arm, Helen administered the injection. Working quickly, carefully, her hands firm, yet gentle, she covered as much of the man's body as she could with the blankets Marsh handed her. While she worked, Helen was aware of the machine being backed into position beside the disabled one, of chains being fixed into place. When Marsh grasped her elbow, she stood up and stepped back.

In a strained hush everyone watched as, motor growling, chains rattling over winches, the shuddering machine was set aright. Whispering, "Oh, God," Helen watched the injured man's leg dangle crookedly over the side of the machine. Then with a barked, "Don't touch him," she stopped the men's move toward him. Marsh beside her, she walked up to that leg.

"Is there a scissors in that box?"

"Yes."

Seconds later Helen was snipping away, quickly, but cautiously, at the blood-soaked material. Her eyes closed briefly when the leg was exposed. The leg was mangled, literally crushed, and with the weight of inadequacy pushing on her mind, she didn't know where to begin. She drew a deep breath, then gave a silent, thankful prayer of relief on hearing the scream of the ambulance siren.

The construction crew guiding the driver, the ambulance was backed as closely as possible to the injured man and two paramedics jumped out and went into action. Working with them, Helen helped cushion and immobilize the leg with an inflatable plastic casing, then the man was moved carefully onto the litter. Strangely

Helen knew one of the paramedics, as she had delivered his first and only child, and after sliding the litter into the long vehicle, he slapped the door shut, smiled, winked, and murmured, "Good work, Doc."

Feeling the praise unearned, Helen nevertheless returned his smile with a soft "Thank you."

As the paramedics climbed back into the ambulance, a hard arm slid around her back.

"I'd like to follow along to the hospital, if you don't mind. There'll be questions to answer, forms to fill out. And I'll have to call Cullen, give him a report on the man's condition."

"Yes, of course. But you do realize it may be some time before any definite word is given out." Breathlessly she moved beside him as, striding along, he half dragged, half carried, her over the rough ground toward her car.

"I know." He gave her a small smile. "But it's got to be done and I've got to do it. The man has no family here."

The drive was a short one, as they took the man to a local hospital. For the following forty-five minutes Helen stood with Marsh as he filled out form after form, answered questions. Helen was asked questions also, but at last it was all finished and the desk nurse said, "If you'd like to wait in the lounge, Doctor, Mr. Kirk, the doctor will have some information for you as soon as possible."

About to walk away, Marsh turned back to the nurse.

"If we're wanted, we'll be in the coffee shop." He paused, then asked, "There is a coffee shop?"

The nurse smiled, nodded, and gave them directions.

"Not exactly what I had in mind when I promised you lunch." Marsh smiled ruefully twenty-five minutes later when the waitress walked away after serving them their food.

"But I love chicken noodle soup." Helen smiled, indicating the steaming bowl in front of her. And with a wave of her hand, over her sandwich, added, "And I've been a cheeseburger freak since I was a kid." She sipped at the cup cradled in her hands. "The coffee is hot and really very good. It's an excellent lunch, Marsh." Her eyes teased him. "And you can't beat the prices."

"You're a cheap date." Marsh's warmly glowing eyes teased back. "Remind me to invite you out to lunch again sometime."

It was after four thirty when they returned to the waiting lounge, and after only a few tense moments Helen suddenly remembered something. Standing up, she held out her hand to Marsh, palm up.

"Give me your car keys."

Without question Marsh stood up, plunged his hand into his pocket, then, glancing up, curiously asked, "What for?"

"I'm going to go for your car," she answered simply. "I'll ask the desk nurse to call a cab for me and go get your car."

"Helen, that's not necessary," Marsh said softly.

"I know." Her eyes were teasing again. "But I hate hanging around hospital waiting rooms. Now give me the keys and the address of the garage and I'll be back before you can even miss me."

"I seriously doubt that," he drawled, dropping the keys into her hand.

It was after six when they finally left the hospital, relief on hearing the man would not lose his leg rendering a spring to their step. Marsh walked Helen to her car, unlocked and opened the door for her before asking, "Can you be ready by eight?"

"Ready for what?"

"For dinner." Marsh grinned. "Maybe a bowl of soup and a cheeseburger would hold you for hours but I have a suspicion that in another hour or so I'm going to be looking forward to a steak. So can you be ready?"

"I'm really very tired, Marsh, and—"

"Nothing fancy," Marsh promised. "And I plan to take you home as soon as we've finished dinner."

Helen was vaguely unsettled by his words, but with a sigh she agreed.

There was nothing fancy about the restaurant Marsh took her to. But it was clean and quiet and the food was delicious and the wine was good.

Later, standing in the hallway in front of her open apartment door, Marsh cupped her face in his hands, kissed her softly.

"You were pretty wonderful today, Helen," he murmured. "Some day, very soon, you and I are going to have a long, serious discussion. But right now you look too tired to think properly, let alone talk." He kissed her again, then dropped his hands. "Go inside, go to bed. I'll call you late in the morning."

Lying in bed, Helen closed her eyes, as if by doing so, she could close out the certainty painfully searing her mind. He was ready to make his move, play his high card, and she knew it. And the knowing hurt, more than she had ever dreamed it would.

CHAPTER 9

By midmorning Sunday Helen had come to terms with her emotions. Although, when embarking on this charade, she had not fully considered the possibly painful ramifications to herself, she could not throw in her hand now. No, pride demanded she play the hand to the last card, then pick up what emotional chips were left and go home.

When Marsh called, Helen was able to talk to him calmly, but she wasn't yet ready to see him. In an easy tone she could hardly believe she'd achieved, she told him she didn't want to go out that afternoon, as she had a hundred personal things she had to catch up on.

"A full hundred?" he mocked. "Are you trying to put off the inevitable, love?"

Helen felt a sinking sensation in the pit of her stomach. Marsh hadn't called her "love" in that tone for weeks. She was right. He was ready for the big play.

Her eyes closed against the renewed pain. She should have felt relieved, thankful that it would be over soon. She didn't. She felt sick, and suddenly very tired.

"Helen?"

She'd been quiet very long. Too long.

"Yes, Marsh."

"Are you all right?" The concern in his voice, which he made no effort to hide, deepened her pain. "I mean, are you feeling all right?"

"Yes, of course." Helen forced a light laugh. "I'm sorry, Marsh, I'm afraid I'm still a little sleep-vacant." Helen winced at the lie. "I haven't been up very long and I don't have the mental process together yet."

"I can't wait to hear what you'll have to say when you get it together." He laughed, then chided, "Do you think you will have your hundred personal chores finished by dinnertime? I'll make reservations somewhere."

Again she hesitated, but only briefly this time.

"All right, Marsh, but I want to have an early night. I'm scheduled for O.R. early tomorrow morning." At least that was the truth.

"Something serious?"

"Yes." She would say no more.

"Okay, love, you're the boss. I'll pick you up at six thirty and you can be back home and tucked in for the night by ten."

Alone, Helen added silently.

The restaurant was a new one for Helen. Spanish in decor, with a lot of black wrought iron complemented by dark red tablecloths and carpet. The menu was a disappointment, being entirely American. The closest Helen got to Spain was the bottle of imported sangría, compliments of the house, that was included with every—expensive—meal.

After dinner Helen played with the stem of her tiny cordial glass, staring at the Tia Maria inside.

"Are you going to admire it or drink it?" Marsh teased.

Startled out of her reverie, Helen glanced up, saw his own Drambuie was gone. A red-jacketed waiter stopped at their table, refilled the coffee cups. When he walked away again, Marsh pinned her with curious eyes.

"Something bothering you, Helen?"

The Game Is Played

"No." Her fingertip circled the rim of the small glass. *You are certainly not playing this very intelligently,* she told herself bleakly. *Perhaps it's time to throw a card that will put him off balance, just a little.* "I was just wondering if you'd care to escort me to a party Saturday night."

"Of course," he replied promptly. "Did you doubt that I would?"

"I wasn't sure." Helen shrugged. "I'm afraid it won't be a very lively affair, but I don't want to miss it."

"What sort of party is it?"

"Retirement." Helen sipped her drink, smiled gently. "My chief in OB. He's a nice man and a brilliant surgeon. I'm going to miss him and I would like to go."

"So we'll go," Marsh said easily, then his eyes narrowed slightly. "But now something bothers me."

"What?" Helen answered warily.

"Why you even hesitated about mentioning it. Did you really think I wouldn't want to go with you?" He paused and his tone grew an edge. "Or were you hating the idea that you'd finally have to introduce me to some of your friends?"

"Marsh!" Helen's shocked tone hid the curl of unease she felt.

"Don't play the innocent with me, love." He rapped softly. "You didn't really think I'd bought those lame excuses, did you? I knew all along why you were dodging that particular issue. Part of it, the biggest part, was this damned hang-up you have about our age difference." He leaned back lazily in his chair; his eyes refuted that laziness. Very softly he warned, "I'm not exactly stupid, you know."

A chill of apprehension trickled down Helen's spine. She was sure he was giving her a definite warning about something—but what? For a brief, panicky second Helen felt sure he knew she was playing him at his own game. Then common sense took over. She had made her position clear from the beginning, had told him bluntly she wanted no involvement of any kind. There was no reason whatever for him to be suspicious. Once again his pride had been touched and he didn't like it. And so the warning; it was as simple as that.

When Marsh didn't pursue the subject, Helen convinced herself her diagnosis was correct.

During the week Helen changed her mind about what to wear for the party at least four times. At one point she even convinced herself she needed something new. Never had she been so nervous about going out somewhere. After long mental arguments she finally scrapped the idea of a new gown. She *had* a new gown. She'd bought it for the holidays and never worn it. And though the calendar said it was just about spring, the temperature said it was still very much winter.

On Saturday night, standing fully dressed in front of her mirror, Helen still wasn't sure of her dress. There was very little of it, at least the top part of it, and Helen wondered for the tenth time if it was right for her. Its cut was deceptively simple, with a rather deep *V* neckline and straight, clingy skirt slit up the right side to the knee. The sleeves were of free-flowing chiffon, almost the same as no covering at all. About the only thing that did please Helen was the shimmery midnight-blue color. Marsh's gift chains were the only jewlery she wore. She had coiled her hair back, telling herself the severe style offset the gown's more daring effect.

"Very elegant."

They were Marsh's first words when she opened the door to him and they echoed her thought about his appearance. In black tux and white ruffled shirt, the only word to describe him was devastating.

The party was being held in the ballroom of one of the city's largest hotels. Helen had not been in the room five minutes before she saw her own opinion of Marsh's looks reflected in the eyes of a dozen women. The sudden mixture of feelings those devouring female eyes sent searing through her made her want to run for the nearest exit. Pride, jealousy, and, Lord help her, possessiveness raged through her like a raging bull gone mad. It made her feel a little sick. It made her feel a little angry. But, worst of all, it made her feel foolish, and that she could not bear.

With a smile on her lips that was pure honey, and tasted in her mouth like straight acid, Helen introduced Marsh to friends as they moved around the room. Helen was aware of more than one pair of eyebrows raised over eyes full of shocked disbelief, and she could imagine what everyone was thinking. She was rarely ever seen with a man, and when she was, it was usually with a close friend who was the husband of a closer friend. People who were her friends knew she simply did not indulge. Now here she was, not only with a man they had never met before, but a younger one as well. Helen had a feeling of certainty that the postparty conversations between husbands and wives would be loaded with speculation.

Marsh seemed sublimely unaware of it all. The glittery, assessing glances from women of varying ages, the raised brows, even the sharp inspection from her chief, apparently went over his head. But Helen saw it, and she didn't like it, not any of it.

Along the one end of the long room a table had been placed for the retiree and his family. In front of that, placed informally, were the other tables. Beyond them a large space had been left clear for dancing, and at the other end a small combo awaited their cue to begin playing. Along the far wall a long buffet table had been set up, and next to that was an almost equally long bar.

Marsh found a table, tucked against a pillar, barely big enough for two and that's where they sat, turning down, with a smile, the numerous offers from friends to join them. Helen knew it was real friendship that prompted the offers, friendship and a big dash of curiosity.

Amii Lorin

After the short speeches were made and the toasts given, the party's planner invited everyone to help himself to the food and the dance floor.

To the background music of a popular new ballad, Marsh asked, "Do you want something to eat or drink?"

"Not yet." Helen shook her head.

"Good, let's dance."

All the way to the dance floor Helen was called to, waved at, but Marsh would not let her stop. A smile on his lips, his hand firmly grasping hers, he kept moving, until, reaching the dancing area, he turned her into his arms with an exaggerated sigh.

"I had no idea you had so many friends," he groaned. "Didn't you mention that only some of your friends would be here tonight?"

"They aren't all close friends, Marsh." Helen laughed softly. "There are quite a few people here I only see at the hospital." Her smile remained, but her tone went dry. "I think you're the one causing all this sudden interest in me."

"I can't imagine why," he drawled. "I'm really very ordinary."

Oh, sure, Helen thought, *about as much as Pavarotti is ordinary compared to other singers.*

An attractive young nurse, a Linda something-or-other, not at all shy or reticent, tapped Helen on the shoulder. Glancing around, Helen's eyes went wide with surprise at the young woman's words.

"Can I cut in, Doctor?" She smiled beautifully. "I was just saying to the girls I'm with that your escort is the best-looking man on the dance floor and—well—they dared me to cut in on you."

Astounded, Helen didn't know what to say until, flicking a glance at Marsh, she saw the amusement tugging at his lips.

"But of course," she purred sweetly. "I was dying for

something to drink anyway." Moving out of Marsh's arms, away from his mocking eyes, she wiggled her fingers at him. "Have fun."

Helen accepted the glass of champagne from the bartender and took a large swallow, her eyes gleaming with fury. *And he says the difference in our ages doesn't matter,* she fumed. She swallowed some more of the wine, then looked at the glass as if seeing it for the first time. *No wonder I feel like a fool,* she thought bitterly, *I am one. And if I'm not careful, in another minute I'll be a smashed fool.*

"Good evening, Helen. It's been a long time."

The deep-timbred voice jerked her mind away from her own shortcomings and her head around to stare into the handsome face of Carl Engle.

"Oh! Hello, Carl." Helen smiled coolly. "You startled me."

"I'm sorry, I didn't mean to." He smiled warmly. "May I get you more wine?"

Helen frowned at the empty glass in her hand. She didn't even remember finishing it.

"Yes, please." Even though she didn't want it, Helen decided she'd look like even more of a fool standing around with an empty glass in her hand.

While Carl spoke to the waiter, then waited for a fresh glass of wine, Helen studied him unobtrusively. She had seen him at various functions over the last few years, but this was the first time she looked, really looked, at him.

There was not a hint of gray in the fair hair that contrasted beautifully with the deep tan on his handsome face. And he had matured into a handsome man, Helen admitted. Tall, still slim, his brown eyes bright and alert, he'd catch the eye of more than his share of females. Helen felt a strange sensation at the thought. If he had exercised some judgment, acquired a little maturity while still in college, he would probably be her husband today. For some unknown reason Helen was very glad he hadn't and wasn't.

"Are you here alone?" He turned back to her, the smile deepening, revealing even white teeth.

"No, I came with—"

"Me." Marsh finished the sentence for her, his eyes somber as they went slowly over Carl.

"Carl Engle, Marshall Kirk." Helen introduced quietly. Marsh's eyes narrowed a fleeting second, but it was the only indication he gave that he'd ever heard the name before. So much, Helen thought wryly, for his saying he'd thank Carl if he ever met him.

Two arms were extended, hands were clasped and almost immediately released.

"Kirk." Carl mused. "Any connection to the accounting firm of Kirk and Terrell?"

"The same Kirk," Marsh answered quietly.

"I've heard some very good things about your firm," Carl murmured. "You're connected with Hannlon Construction also, aren't you?"

"My grandfather," Marsh admitted.

"I know your sister, Kristeen," Carl said, then smiled at Marsh's raised brows. "I'm your niece's pediatrician." Before Marsh could reply, Carl smiled at Helen. "Another patient to thank you for, Dr. Cassidy."

"The choice is theirs." Helen shrugged. "If they ask for a recommendation, I supply three names."

"Well, thank you for including me in the three." Carl laughed. "Now, as the saying goes, may I have the next dance?"

"Excuse me," Marsh inserted before Helen could think of a polite way of saying no. "I promised Helen I'd take her to the buffet as soon as that dance was finished."

"Of course," Carl replied. "Maybe later."

Marsh smiled thinly in answer, grasped Helen's arm, and led her toward the end of the long table.

"I distinctly remember telling you I was not hungry," Helen chided coolly.

"I distinctly remember you telling me you were not thirsty," Marsh retorted, one eyebrow arched at her half-empty glass.

They ate in silence, Helen picking disinterestedly at the small amount of food on her plate. When Marsh had cleaned off his plate, he tossed his napkin on top of it and pinned her with very cool blue eyes.

"Did you want to dance with him?" His tone was cold and, Helen thought, somehow condemning. Her hackles rose.

"Would it have mattered if I did?" She didn't wait for him to answer, adding sweetly, "Did you enjoy your dance?"

Watching his eyes narrow, Helen felt sick. Even to herself she sounded like a jealous, possessive woman.

"Not particularly," he finally answered. "I'm not turned on by gushy, clingy females."

"Too bad," she purred, looking beyond him. "There's another, probably the gushiest, heading this way. I imagine they'll all ask you now."

Helen recognized the girl coming toward them, for it was the student who had referred to Marsh as "totally bad" on the day Helen met him.

When she stopped at their table, Marsh stood up, a charmingly polite smile on his lips.

"Oh, Mr. Kirk." The girl actually did gush. "Doctor, I hope you don't mind, but Linda will be unbearable for the rest of the night if the rest of us don't get a dance."

"How many are the rest of you?" Marsh asked warily.

"Four," the girl answered brightly. "Including me."

Helen saw Marsh's lips tighten, but before he could say a word, she laughed softly. "Four's not many. Go along, Marsh." She dismissed him airily. "I'm perfectly happy here . . . by myself."

Marsh made a motion with his hand for the girl to

precede him, then before following her, he turned a thunderous look on Helen. "You'll pay for this, woman," he whispered harshly.

Helen watched his retreating back, deriving a malicious pleasure in the stiffness of it. He certainly didn't like being manipulated.

"Time for that dance now, Helen?" Carl stood beside her, an expectant smile on his face.

"Yes, thank you." Helen smiled, thinking, *Well, why not? Anything's better than sitting here like the proverbial wallflower.*

Carl had always been a good dancer, smooth, easy to follow, and after a few minutes Helen felt some of the angry tautness leave her.

"You've matured into a beautiful woman, Helen." Carl's voice was low, oddly urgent.

A tiny smile touching her lips at his unknowing echo of her earlier thoughts about him, she glanced up.

"Thank you."

"Have you ever forgiven me, Helen?" he asked abruptly.

Helen's glance wavered, then grew steady again. "There's nothing to forgive, for nothing really happened." *No actual rape that is,* she amended mentally, *only two blows, the second with your fist.* "I never think of it." She lied. *Then what,* she chided herself, *were you sobbing about in Marsh's arms that night?*

"We could have made it together."

"What?" His incredible words shocked her out of her thoughts.

"You and I," he explained softly. "We could have made it very good." He drew her a little closer, and amazed at his cool presumption, Helen didn't resist. In fact she was hardly aware of him, for she had just caught a glimpse of Marsh with yet another girl in his arms, a little older, much prettier than the others.

"We still could, Helen." The urgent voice tried to draw her attention.

"How?" Helen wasn't even sure of what he was saying. All she was sure of was the hot jealousy running through her veins and the sick shame that jealousy spawned.

"Don't be naive, darling." Carl's lips touched her hair as he brought her closer still. "My wife would never know, and even if she did, I doubt if she'd care."

His lips, as well as his words, brushing her ear, brought her alert. She knew his wife and had heard of the number of mistresses he'd had.

"I find that a little hard to believe," she said carefully.

"You needn't, I assure you." Again his arms tightened, and Helen felt anger replace her jealousy. "My wife's a little girl playing house. Only in her case the dolls are our children and the playhouse furniture is life-sized. As long as her little domain is not threatened, she couldn't care less what I do." He paused then added fatuously, "You do understand, I have no intention of threatening that domain."

Of course not, Helen thought furiously, *you're not stupid. Why lose the goodwill of a very prominent and influential father-in-law, if you can have your cake and eat it*. Helen placed her hands on his chest, about to push him away while she told him exactly what she thought of him. She didn't get a chance to do either.

"May I cut in?" Marsh's voice was low, deceptively quiet. "I believe you promised me this dance, Helen." His arm slid around her waist, his fingers gripped painfully.

"Yes, of course." Helen was suddenly breathless with apprehension. Good Lord, she couldn't allow him to make a scene *here*. "And then, if you don't mind, I'd like to go home."

Amii Lorin

Marsh nodded, started to turn her away, but Carl, seeming to think her words were a good sign for him, said softly, "I'll call you, Helen."

"No, you won't."

Flat, final, the words hung between the two men like a sword. Marsh's eyes cold, detached, bored into Carl's. Carl's dropped first as, with a shrug, he smile faintly and walked away.

"Marsh, really, you—"

"Be quiet, Helen." Marsh's tone matched his eyes for coldness. "Do you want to dance or do you want to go home?"

"I—" Helen drew a deep breath. "I think we'd better go."

Without a word he turned on his heel, grasped her arm, and headed for the door. After hasty farewells to their host Helen found herself rushed to the cloakroom. Marsh asked for his car to be brought around, and as they stepped out of the door Helen gasped. There was at least three inches of snow on the ground and it was still coming down hard.

Driving was bad, requiring all Marsh's concentration, and the distance to her apartment was covered in silence. Helen could feel his anger beating against her like storm-tossed waves. Knowing there would be a confrontation when they got to her place, Helen almost dreaded arriving home. To her surprise he did not drive onto the parking lot, but pulled up, motor running, under the marquee that protected the entrance. She hesitated a second but when he didn't speak or even look at her, she slid across the seat, got out, closed the door carefully, and ran into the building.

Inside her apartment Helen went straight to her bedroom. She was wearing thin-strap evening sandals and her feet had gotten soaked in her short dash through the snow to the car. Now she felt chilled to the bone, not only from her foot soaking. She stripped, then took a arms, dancing, did you find you still feel something for him?"

"No." It was stated simply, positively, but it didn't satisfy him.

"Then why did you allow him to practically crawl all over you?" he snapped. "What was he saying to you?"

Helen could have cried aloud. She didn't want to answer him. He was mad enough already. She hesitated a moment. It was a moment too long.

"Answer me, Helen." He gave her a little shake. "What did he say?"

"He suggested an . . . arrangement." She sighed. "He also assured me his wife would not interfere. You men are wonderful creatures, aren't you?" she ended bitterly.

A flame flared in Marsh's eyes. "It takes two to play that kind of game. A man *and* a woman." His fingers dug into her arms. "What did you tell him?"

"I wanted to tell him to go to hell." Helen's eyes flashed back at him. "But you showed up before I could."

Helen could actually see the anger seep out of him. His face became less rigid; his fingers relaxed their punishing hold.

"If he calls you," he spat out, "or tries to see you—"

"I'm sure he won't," Helen said quickly, feeling his fingers tighten again. "I think you made it very clear that he shouldn't."

"He'd better not." He drew her closer, his fingers loosening again, massaging her tender skin. Then her eyes widened as he breathed softly, "You're mine, Helen. And the game is over."

"No, I'm—"

His mouth caught her parted lips, silencing her. If the kiss had been rough or hard, she could have fought him. It was neither. Gently, tenderly, his mouth put his stamp of ownership on her. Melting, trembling, she felt his hand slide down her back, his arm gather her tightly to him.

hot shower, slipped into her nightgown and quilted, belted robe, and started for the kitchen to make a cup of tea.

The doorbell's ring stopped her in the kitchen doorway. Now who in the world? Helen glanced at the clock. At this hour? The ring came again, short, angry sounding. Helen walked slowly to the door, checked to see if the chain was in place, then opened the door two inches.

Marsh stood in the hall looking every bit as angry as he had when he'd dropped her off less than forty-five minutes ago. He also looked the tough construction worker he'd once been, dressed in a suede, fur-lined jacket, brushed-denim jeans, and what looked like logging boots laced almost to the knee.

"What do you want?" Slipping the chain, Helen stepped back. He walked in far enough to close the door. One eyebrow arched mockingly.

"There are a few questions I want answers to." He slipped out of his jacket.

"But why didn't you ask them when you brought me home?" She moved away from him edgily.

"I wanted to get the car home." He bent over, began unlacing his boots.

"But—"

"I have one of the company's four-wheel-drive pickups," he answered before she could ask. After tugging the boots off, he padded across the room to her. His eyes were cool, direct.

"Do you still feel something for him?"

Helen gasped. She didn't know what she'd been expecting, but it certainly hadn't been that.

"Carl?"

The confusion in her tone seemed to anger him even more. Grasping her shoulders painfully, he pulled her close to him.

"Yes, Carl," he gritted through clenched teeth. "While you were in his arms." His lips twisted, his tone grew sarcastic. "While you were held so very closely in his

His mouth left hers, moved slowly across her cheek to her ear.

"Helen, Helen." The voice that whispered her name was raw. "Oh, God, I love you. Hold me, love. Please hold me."

Helen's arms slid up and around his neck, and she closed her eyes against the quick hot sting inside. Turning her face into the side of his neck, she breathed in deeply. His cologne, plus the male scent of him, confused her thinking.

"Marsh," she whispered, trying to hang on to her evaporating reason. "You—we shouldn't."

"Yes, we should." His warm breath feathered her ear, tickled its way down the length of her body. "We should have long ago."

His mouth left a fiery trace over her face, back to her lips. And now she was ready for the driving force that crushed her mouth, made dust of her resistance. Tiny little sparks burst into flames inside her. Flames that leaped higher and higher as his mouth grew more demanding.

Her own hunger aroused, Helen returned his kiss, barely aware of what he was doing, when she felt his hands loosen her belt, pull her arms down, slide her robe off. But she was aware of his hands moving over the silky material of her nightgown, was aware of the sudden need to feel those hands against her skin. The awareness brought momentary sanity. Tearing her mouth from his, she gasped for air, finally found her voice.

"Marsh, no." Helen couldn't breath properly and she paused to draw a short, shallow breath. She shuddered as his lips nibbled along the strained cord in her neck. "Oh, Marsh, no." It was a feeble protest against his hands sliding the gown's narrow straps from her shoulders. The gown slid to the floor silently, and then Helen's body became electrically charged at the touch of his hands. His lips found the beginning swell of her breasts and she moaned softly. Moving lazily, the tip of his tongue driving the flame yet higher, his mouth retraced the trail to her lips. Reason was gone, common sense was gone; all that was left was the ache to be with him. Sliding her arms around his neck, she dug her fingers into his hair. Lifting his head, he stared down at her, his breathing ragged.

"Sweet Lord, I can't wait anymore," he whispered hoarsely. "I won't wait anymore."

Bending swiftly, he swung her up into his arms and carried her into the bedroom. He laid her gently onto the bed, then straightened, his eyes caressing her as he pulled his silky knit sweater over his head and tossed it into a corner. When his hand went to the snap at the waistband of his jeans, Helen closed her eyes. He was beside her in seconds, his skin warm and firm against hers. "Marsh, I—"

"I love you," he whispered fiercely, his mouth closing off any further protests from her. His hands brought every inch of her skin tinglingly alive, his mouth drove her to the edge of madness. Aching, moaning deep in her throat, she opened her eyes wide when he ordered, "Tell me you love me."

"I love you," she repeated weakly.

"Again."

"I love you." A little stronger this time.

"Again."

"I love you. I love you. Damn you, I love you."

"Good." Blatant satisfaction coated his tone.

Her nails punished him, but he laughed softly. "You have a hunger almost as great as mine, love." He kissed her, his tongue probing until she arched uncontrollably against him.

"What do you want, love?" he teased.

"Don't," she pleaded.

"Tell me what you want," he demanded relentlessly.

"You," she sobbed. "I want you. Don't torture me, Marsh, please."

"Torture? You don't know the meaning of the word." His lips teased hers, the tip of his tongue ran along the outline of her upper lip. "I wanted to hear you say it, Helen. I had to hear it." His body shifted, blanketing hers, and with a whispered, but definite "Now," his lips ceased their teasing, became hard, urgent.

It was everything a younger Helen had once hoped it would be. And much, much more than her imagination had ever dared hope for. Slowly, gently, Marsh guided her through the first fleeting moments of discomfort, then, his passion unleashed, he introduced her to a world she'd never dreamed existed. A world of pure sensation, of tension almost unbearable, of pleasure so exquisite that it held a thread of pain. Finer, yet more defined, the sweet bud of agony slowly blossomed. When it burst into full bloom there was soaring joy, shuddering victory, and one brief moment of unconsciousness that filled Helen with wonder. And the most incredible thing was that the near perfection could be repeated, as Marsh proved at regular intervals, over and over again. It was after four in the morning before Marsh, with a softly taunted "Quitter," let her drift into sleep.

The eerie silence that smothers the world with a heavy snowfall woke Helen late in the morning. Without moving, she opened her eyelids slowly. The space on the bed beside her was empty. Turning her head, her eyes came to his tall form, standing in front of the window. Barely breathing, she studied that form, a sharp pain stabbing at her heart. He had pulled on his jeans, but nothing else, and with his fingers tucked into his back pockets, his muscles bunched tautly in his arms across his shoulders. Head up, somber-faced, he stared out through the window, a quality of waiting about him.

Waiting for what? To laugh? To crow over his triumph? To be prepared to smile indulgently as she meekly accepted his terms? Helen squirmed inwardly at her own thoughts, hating herself for her own weakness—almost hating him for taking advantage of that weakness.

Her eyes closed again, covering the pain and despair he could have easily read had he turned his head. She knew what she looked like in the morning. She faced that reality every day. Face pale, tiny lines of strain and years around her eyes and mouth. And this morning she would look even worse with her hair a tangled mess framing her pale face.

Helen would have been more shocked had someone thrust a mirror in front of her, forced her to open her eyes. The afterglow of love still tinged her cheeks; the tiny lines of strain had smoothed out, been partially erased by the release of tension; and the disarray of her hair gave her an untamed, sensual look. In essence the image she would have seen reflected in a mirror, and that Marsh did see when he turned his head, was of a breath-catchingly beautiful woman. But no one did place a mirror in front of her, and Helen was convinced, on opening her eyes and finding Marsh's brooding ones on her, that what those hooded eyes observed displeased him.

Unable to bear those unreadable eyes on her, the taut, waiting stillness that held him, her hands curled into tight, determined fists under the covers. He had played his ace to her king, but if he thought he had won the game he was in for a shock. She still held one card and she would let *him* squirm awhile before she played it. The veneer of cool professionalism was pulled into place. In a voice withdrawn, detached from all the happenings of the past night, Helen clipped, "Are you happy now? Are you satisfied?"

CHAPTER 10

Marsh didn't move. A flame leaped brightly in his blue eyes, then was instantly, deliberately, quenched.

"Am I satisfied?" His voice, devoid of emotion, had a frighteningly dead sound. "For the moment yes. Am I happy? Now? No."

Well, Helen thought dismally, you certainly couldn't argue with a statement as definite as that. It wasn't quite what she had expected, but then, when had he ever done anything quite like she'd expected?

"Helen, about last night—"

No! a voice screamed inside her head. No, she would not listen to terms or possible plans or—maybe—rejection, not while she still lay on the battlefield of her own defeat.

"Marsh," she interrupted quickly. "I want to have a shower, get dressed." Dragging the sheet with her, she sat up.

"Helen," Marsh gritted impatiently, "we have got to talk about—"

"Marsh, please." She again cut him off. "Will you leave this room so I can get up?"

His body stiffened, and she could see the battle that

raged inside him. Then, with a curt nod, he turned and strode across the room, scooping his sweater off the floor in passing, and left the room, closing the door with an angry snap.

Fighting the urge to run after him, to agree to everything and anything he wanted, Helen slid off the bed and ran into the bathroom.

Twenty minutes later he walked into the kitchen to face him, her resolve strengthened, her course clearly mapped out in her mind.

He had made a pot of coffee and stood leaning against the counter, a cup of steaming brew cradled in his hands. Her small kitchen radio played softly in the background. When she entered the room, he set down his cup, filled a matching one for her, handed it to her, then tilted his head at the only window in the room.

"I've just heard a weather report," he said quietly. "We had over a foot of snow during the night and it's still snowing heavily. The weather bureau is calling for another three to five inches."

A very safe subject, Helen thought cynically, the weather. Falling in with his lead, she murmured, "Driving is going to be a nightmare. It's a good thing you took your car home."

He nodded and polished off half his coffee in several swallows. The subject of the weather exhausted, a strained, uneasy silence vibrated between them. They both jumped at the sudden, discordant ring from the phone. Helen snatched up the receiver on the second ring, beating her service to it.

"Dr. Cassidy."

"Doctor, this is David Stewart. My wife fell a little while ago and is in labor." The man rushed all in one breath. Gasping quickly, he hurried on. "What the hell am I going to do? I can't even get my car out of the garage."

Conjuring up a mental picture of Cheryl Stewart, Helen asked calmly, "How far apart are the contractions?"

"I don't know," he answered distractedly, then, "just a minute, my mother-in-law is timing it now." There was a short pause, then, "Five minutes, Doctor."

"Mr. Stewart, give me your address, then go hold your wife's hand." Helen's calm voice soothed. "I'll send an ambulance out and meet you at the hospital."

"But can an ambulance get out here in this mess?" His voice was now frantic. Hearing an outcry of pain in the background, Helen knew why. This was the Stewarts' first baby.

"I'm sure it can, Mr. Stewart, if you get off the line and let me call for one."

The line went dead. A small smile pulling at her lips, Helen put through the call for an ambulance. The dispatcher's harried "As soon as possible, Doctor" erased the smile, triggered a curl of unease. Her face thoughtful, Helen replaced the receiver. Glancing around at Marsh, she tossed the address at him.

"Can you get me out there?"

"Yes." He caught on at once. "You don't feel right about this?"

"I'm probably running you on a wild-goose chase." Helen smiled apologetically. "But no, I don't feel right about it."

"So jump into your boots, grab your coat, and let's go." He was already moving toward the living room.

Helen did exactly as he suggested. Less than ten minutes later, ready to go out the door, Helen paused, turned back to Marsh.

"In the closet, at the far end of the shelf, there's a black bag. Will you get it for me, please?"

Walking to the elevator, bag in his hand, Marsh lifted a questioning eyebrow at Helen.

"I don't even know what made me think of it. I've

173

never used it," she explained softly. "My father gave it to me when I entered premed." She hesitated, a gentle smile curving her lips. "He had hoped I'd follow him into general practice."

As Helen had predicted earlier, driving was a nightmare. Even with the four-wheel drive, negotiating the truck through the heavy wet snow required all Marsh's concentration, and as Helen was busy with her own thoughts, the drive was completed in near silence. When Marsh turned onto the street where the Stewarts lived, Helen sighed with a mixture of relief and disappointment. She had hoped to see an ambulance, if only the retreating lights of one, but the street was empty, the snow virgin, smooth.

As he parked the truck Marsh grunted, "At least a path's been shoveled to the curb." Stepping out, he advised, "Slide under the wheel and get out this side."

David Stewart had the door open before they were halfway up the walk.

"Where the hell is that ambulance, Doctor?" His voice was heavy with strain, his face pale. "Her pains are getting closer."

"They'll get here as soon as they can." Helen's tone was soothing as she walked into the small foyer. She removed her coat, then went still at the outcry of a woman in pain. "Where is she? I'll—"

"I don't think this baby is going to wait for an ambulance. Come with me, Doctor."

Helen moved automatically toward the older woman who stood in an archway that led off the living room. Without another word the woman turned and led the way along a short hallway and into a bedroom. Cheryl Stewart lay on the bed, her face drawn with pain, her brow wet with sweat.

"Oh, Doctor," she gasped. "I'm so glad to see you. The pains are very bad."

"She's been very good up until now, Doctor," Cheryl's

mother offered. "I managed to get a plastic sheet and towels under her before her water broke."

Drawing the covering sheet away, Helen nodded her approval. It required the briefest examination to ascertain the truth of the older woman's statement. This baby was not going to wait for anything. Cheryl gasped with the onslaught of another contraction, and Helen urged, "Don't fight it, Cheryl, go with it."

About to call to Marsh to bring her bag, Helen smiled in gratitude when he placed it beside her, asking, "What can I do to help?"

"I think there's a packaged pair of gloves in there. Will you get them for me?"

After that she simply had to ask for what she wanted and it was handed to her. Sheets were draped, tentlike, over the girl's legs, and speaking quietly, encouragingly, Helen delivered the baby.

"Stop pushing now," Helen instructed Cheryl when she held the baby's head and one shoulder in her hands. Then to Marsh, "The syringe ready?"

"Right here" came the calm reply.

Guiding the small form with her hands, Helen drew the baby into the world, then taking the syringe Marsh handed her, she cleaned the tiny mouth and nostrils of birth mucus. The infant sputtered, then began to cry, and Helen placed the red-faced child on Cheryl's stomach.

"You have a beautiful son, Cheryl," she told the exhausted girl.

When she was satisfied that the baby was breathing spontaneously, Helen cut the lifeline cord, unaware that the ambulance had arrived or that the two attendants waited in the hall to take over.

They entered the room as she swabbed the blood from the baby's face.

"Okay, let's go," Helen ordered briskly, wrapping the baby up warmly while the attendants carefully covered Cheryl. "I'll suture in the hospital. Marsh, if you'll follow behind with Mr. Stewart, I'll ride in the ambulance."

Marsh nodded, holding her coat for her, and as she slipped into it he whispered, "That was beautiful, Helen. You're fantastic."

It had stopped snowing and the streets were in somewhat better condition by the time they returned to the Stewart house several hours later. After dropping off a much happier-looking David, Marsh suggested they go to his apartment for something to eat.

"No, Marsh." Helen shook her head firmly. "There's plenty of food in my fridge. Besides which, I need a shower. I'm tired. I want to go home and get comfortable." She didn't bother to add that her tiredness stemmed more from her lack of sleep the night before than the events of the day. She wasn't quite ready to tackle that subject yet.

After a relaxing shower Helen prepared a quick meal of canned soup and bacon, lettuce, and tomato sandwiches. Although they kept the conversation light and general while they ate, Helen could feel the tension of the morning tautening between them again. When the supper things were cleared away, they carried their coffee into the living room. Coffee cup in hand, Marsh paced back and forth for several minutes, then came to an abrupt halt in front of Helen.

"Can we talk now?"

"There is nothing to talk about." Glancing up, Helen saw his lips tighten.

"Last night was nothing?" he asked sharply.

"I didn't say that." Helen stood up, walked to the window. Her back to him, she said, "What I meant was, it doesn't change anything."

"Really?" Marsh mocked dryly. "I'd have thought it changed everything." A small smile replaced the mockery on his lips. "Helen, I told you at the beginning that my intentions were honorable. I'm asking you to marry me."

"No," Helen answered at once, afraid to give herself time to think, to weaken. "It wouldn't work. My life suits me just as it is. I want no commitments, no strings."

"All right, we'll play it your way." His smile deepened as he slowly crossed the room to her. "We'll live together without ceremony. You can move into my place or"—at her frown—"I'll move in here." He shrugged, coming to a stop before her. "It doesn't matter where, as long as I know that when you leave the office or the hospital or wherever, you'll be coming home to me. There'll be no commitments, no strings, no pressures, I promise."

"No, Marsh." Feeling sick, Helen watched the smile leave his face, his eyes narrow.

"I believe you said you love me last night," he said quietly.

"That admission was forced out of me," Helen snapped.

"And that changes it?" he snapped back. "I also believe I told you I love you—at least fifty times."

"And *I'm* positive you believe it—now." Helen backed away from the sudden flare in his eyes. "And I'm positive you believe you could be content with the arrangement you've suggested." Holding up her hand to prevent him from interrupting, she hurried on. "But I'm also very positive that the day would come when that arrangement would not be enough, when you'd ask for more, and I'm not prepared to play the three traditional roles. Not even for you."

"What are you talking about?" Marsh was obviously confused. "What three roles?"

Her heart feeling like a lead weight in her chest, Helen looked him squarely in the eyes and coldly, flatly, threw down her ace of trump.

"The cook in your kitchen, the madonna in your nursery, the mistress in your bed. For whether you believe it now or not, Marsh, I'm positive that the day will come when you'll come home hungry at dinnertime and I won't be here, either to make a meal or go out with you for one, and you'll resent it. And I don't need that."

"Helen."

"And the nights will come," Helen went on, as if he hadn't spoken, "when, after I've been called out, you'll lay alone on the bed and the dissatisfaction will grow. And I don't need that."

"Helen."

There was a low, angry warning in his tone now, and yet Helen went on.

"And the day will surely come when the desire for an extension of yourself, in the form of a child, will bring that resentment and dissatisfaction to an angry confrontation. *And I don't need that.*"

Finished now, Helen stood before him, waiting for his reaction. Finally, when she was beginning to think he would not reply at all, he said softly, "In other words you don't need me. Is that what you're saying?"

Helen's throat closed painfully, but telling herself she had to say it, she lifted her head, pushed the word out.

"Yes."

His face went pale and for one flashing instant seemed to contort with pain. In that instant Helen thought she saw raw agony in his eyes, then his head snapped up arrogantly, his jaw hardened, and his eyes went dead.

"Well, that's clear enough." His tone was devoid of expression. "I won't bother you again, Helen."

Fingers curled into her hand, nails digging into her palm, Helen stared into the empty space where he'd stood. Eyes hot with a sudden sting, she heard him stamp into his boots, open the door. Teeth biting down hard on her lip, she kept herself from crying out to him to stop.

Let him go, she silently wept. *Now the game is played.*

For the following two weeks Helen worked at a grueling pace. When she wasn't at the hospital or in the office, she attended every lecture offered—on her own subject of OB–GYN as well as others. She spent as little time as possible in her apartment and saw nothing at all of her friends. Telling herself that the empty, dead feeling inside would pass more quickly if she kept herself busy, she kept busy for all she was worth.

She had just returned home from the hospital on Monday night, two weeks after she had sent Marsh away, when she answered her doorbell and found Kris in the hall.

"I'm sorry to bother you so late, Helen," she apologized after Helen had asked her to come in, "but I've been here several times in the last couple of days and you've always been out."

"I've been rather busy," Helen said warily. "What did you want to see me about?" Helen knew, of course. She hoped she was wrong, but she wasn't.

"Marsh," Kris answered bluntly.

"Kris, I don't—" Helen began.

"Helen, I don't know what happened between you two and I have no intention of asking. But I love him and I'm worried about him and there's something I think you should know."

Helen had continued to stand after asking Kris to sit down, but now, fear whispering through her mind, her legs suddenly weak, she sank onto a chair.

"Worried about him? Why? What's wrong with him?"

"I don't know if anything is," Kris answered distractedly. "Oh, let me explain. Two weeks ago today I took the baby over to Mother's and went shopping. When I returned, I heard voices from the library, and as the door was partially open, I thought Mother was probably in there with Dad, so I walked toward it. Just before I reached the door, the voices became louder and I stopped." Kris wet her lips. "I did not mean to eavesdrop, but I was so shocked by what I heard, I couldn't seem to move."

"Kris," Helen inserted quickly, "if you overheard a private family conversation, I don't think you should be repeating it."

"I have to, Helen," Kris pleaded, "so you'll understand why I'm here." Helen started to shake her head, but Kris rushed on. "I heard my father say to Marsh, 'What do you intend? Good Lord, Son, this woman has an excellent reputation. Are you going to marry her?' I would have moved on then, Helen, really I would. But the odd sound of Marsh's voice kept me motionless. 'She doesn't want me' was all he answered then, but he sounded so strange."

"Kris, please." Helen stood up again, moved around restlessly.

"Then Dad asked him what he was going to do, or something like that." Kris went on relentlessly. "And Marsh almost shouted at him." Kris bit her lip. "Helen, I've never heard Marsh raise his voice to my father before. Still in that odd tone he said, 'I don't know. Right now I'm bleeding to death inside and I simply don't care.' He walked out of the room then and right by me, as if I weren't there. When he got to the door, I called to him, asked him where he was going. He turned and looked through me. Then he smiled very gently and said, 'Very probably to hell.' "

Helen felt as if something had given way inside, and she sat down again very quickly.

"That was the last any of us saw of him. We haven't heard a word from him and have no idea where he is. I know Mother is very upset, and although he doesn't say anything, Dad's beginning to worry too. But there is one person who may know where he is."

Cullen. The name flashed into Helen's mind at the same moment Kris said, "My grandfather. I've been to see him, but all he'll tell me is Marsh can take care of himself and I'm not to worry."

"Then don't," Helen advised, now more than a little concerned herself.

"Oh, Helen," Kris sighed. "How does one not worry about the welfare of someone they love? I can't help but worry. This is just not like Marsh." She hesitated, then suggested tentatively, "If you went to Grandfather, I think he might tell you."

"I can't do that, Kris." Helen was out of her chair again. "I—I have no right to question your grandfather about Marsh."

"Just think about it, please." Kris stood up and walked to the door. "I must go. Mike is waiting in the car." Before she walked out of the door, she urged, "At least think about it, Helen."

"I can't, Kris," was all Helen could find to say.

Three days later Helen stood in front of the large door of the imposing edifice Cullen Hannlon called home. Kris had called her at the office that afternoon to inform her that there had still been no word from Marsh. Unable to bear her own fears and uncertainties any longer, Helen had come to the house directly from the office.

The door was opened by a pleasant-faced woman close to Cullen's own age. Helen asked to see Mr. Hannlon, then gave her name and was ushered inside and along a wide beautifully paneled hall so swiftly that she almost felt she had been expected. The woman stopped at a door midway down the hall, tapped lightly, then pushed the door open and motioned Helen inside.

Cullen Hannlon stood beside a long narrow window, a smile on his still-handsome face.

"Ah, Helen, come in, come in," he urged. "I've been standing here enjoying the sunshine. This more springlike weather feels so good after that snow a few weeks ago. But come, sit down. Can I get you some coffee or a drink?"

"No, nothing, thank you," Helen murmured, wondering where to begin. "Mr. Hannlon, I—I—"

"Kris has been talking to you, hasn't she?" He smiled knowingly. "I was afraid she would."

"Do you know where he is?" Helen asked bluntly.

"Yes." He was equally blunt. "But I can't tell you. I gave him my word."

"But—"

"No, Helen, I'm sorry." He really did sound sorry; he also sounded adamant. "I don't know what the problem is, but I do know my grandson's hurting. He went away on my suggestion and with my word that I'd tell no one where he is. I don't think you would ask me to break my word to him."

"No," Helen whispered. "Of course not."

"But I can tell you this," he said gently. "He will be back within two weeks. Should I tell him you were here?" This last was added hopefully.

Helen rose quickly. "No, please don't. I need some time myself." She paused, then admitted, to herself as well as him, "To reorganize my thinking."

I love him. Nothing has changed that; nothing ever will.

Helen lost count of the times she faced that fact during the next two weeks. With a suddenness that was shattering, she realized that without him her work, her independence, everything she had counted as precious, had very little meaning to her. She longed to see him, feel his strong arms draw her close against his hard body. It was spring and she wanted to walk in the park with him. She didn't hear a word from, or about, him.

Toward the end of that week Helen had a rough delivery. Rough in two ways. The breech birth in itself was difficult. The fact that her patient was her oldest and closest friend made it doubly so.

She had first met Estelle while in her first year of premed. Being the daughter of Helen's favorite professor, Estelle had been at home the first time Helen had been invited to his house. They had very few similar interests, and yet they became fast friends. The friendship had endured the years.

Estelle, scatterbrained and happy-go-lucky, surprised everyone, except possibly Helen, by marrying a serious-minded English professor ten years her senior. Everyone said the union could not possibly work. Everyone was wrong. Estelle and John balanced each other perfectly. There was only one unhappy note in their marriage: Estelle's inability to carry a child full term. After her third miscarriage, at the age of thirty-one, Estelle was strongly advised by Helen not to get pregnant again.

Estelle, being Estelle, disregarded Helen's advice and came to her two years later to confirm her pregnancy. And Helen, being Helen, was determined to see this child born. And now, after a pregnancy spent almost entirely in bed, a very long, hard labor, and an extremely difficult delivery, Helen smiled with joy at both mother and son.

The new father was gently adoring when he was allowed a few minutes with his exhausted wife, proud as a prancing stallion when he viewed his offspring, and full of praise when he rejoined Helen in the waiting lounge.

"I want to buy you dinner." He grinned as he crossed the room to her. "I want to buy you champagne." Pulling her to him, he gave her a bear hug. "God, Helen, I want to buy you the moon."

"I'll settle for dinner," Helen told him solemnly, her eyes teasing.

He picked the most expensive restaurant in one of the largest hotels. As they had no reservations, they were informed they could be served if they didn't mind a short wait. His high spirits undaunted, John told the maître d' they'd be in the bar and led Helen to it. Some forty-five minutes later they were called to their table. Told they should take their drinks with them, they left the bar drinks in hand. Crossing the threshold into the dining room, Helen came to a jarring stop.

Coming toward her, a lovely, young brunet on his

arm, was the man Helen had spent almost four weeks being sick over. In the few seconds it took for Marsh and the girl to come up to her, Helen noted detail. Marsh looked well, relaxed, and, as he was smiling, happy. The girl, chattering away, looked equally happy. And why not? Helen asked herself bitterly. The girl's left hand rested on his forearm and on the ring finger rested a diamond solitaire big enough to choke a small horse.

The advantage was Helen's, as she had time to compose her features. Smiling down at the girl, Marsh didn't see her until he was practically on top of her.

"Good evening, Helen."

Nothing registered on his face. No emotion, nothing. Helen went him one better—she smiled. "Marsh."

Marsh's cool blue eyes swept their glasses, then Helen's and John's smiling faces.

"A celebration?" His tone was mildly curious.

"Of the best kind," John answered for her. "This beautiful woman has just made me the happiest man in the state."

Helen didn't bother to correct the wrong impression John had given.

"Congratulations," Marsh said dryly, his eyes mocking Helen and the words she'd spoken against marriage just a few weeks before.

"Thank you." John grinned, accepting Marsh's good wishes at face value.

"Excuse me." The brunet's voice was soft but insistent. "Marsh, we have to go. I don't want to be late for my own engagement party."

"Of course," Marsh said at once, then with a brief nod at Helen and John, he led the girl from the room.

Three hours later, pacing back and forth on her living room carpet, Helen was still amazed at the way she'd handled herself. Not only had she eaten her dinner, she had laughed and held up her end of the conversation.

Now she wasn't at all sure her dinner would stay down and she was a great deal closer to tears than laughter. In an effort to keep the tears from escaping, she whipped herself into a rage.

You are not only a fool, she silently stormed, *you're an absolute nitwit. For weeks you've been dragging yourself from day to day, aching for the sight of him. Like an innocent child you talked yourself into believing every word he said. Convinced yourself your life was pointless without him. While he's out getting engaged to a young girl.*

Hands clenched into fists, she paced. Never had she known such anger. Anger at Marsh? Anger at herself? Her mind tried to shy away from the questions, not quite ready to face the final, self-commitment. With no place left to hide, exposed to herself, her mind screamed, *Dammit, he is mine.*

When the doorbell pealed, Helen swung blazing eyes to the door. It was Marsh. She knew it and she was tempted to ignore it. When it rang again, she strode across the room, flipped the lock, and yanked the door open. Without a word Marsh stormed by her, tossed his suit coat at a chair, then, eyes blazing as hotly as hers, turn to confront her.

"Who the hell is he?" he rasped harshly.

"None of your damned business," Helen snapped.

Biting off a curse, Marsh closed the space between them. Grasping her shoulders, he pulled her against his body with such force the air exploded from her lungs.

"It is my damned business," he snarled. "You are mine, Helen." He jerked his head in the direction of the bedroom. "I made you mine in there. Now get on that phone and call what's-his-name and tell him to run along. He can't have you."

Sheer fury ripped through Helen. Of all the arrogant swine. Talk about wanting to have your cake and eat it all at the same time. He actually came from his own engagement party to tell her she belonged to him and couldn't have another man.

Twisting out of his arms, she spun away from him, then spun back, her voice icy.

"You—you . . . boy." She flung at him. "Get out of here before I hit you." Incensed, raging, no longer thinking, she cried, "To think I went to that old man."

"You went to Cullen? Why?"

She was long past noticing how still he'd grown, how tight was his tone.

"To find out where you were." Helen was near to shouting. She didn't care. Her laughter was not pretty. "I was ready to crawl on my knees to you. I must have been out of my—"

She was pulled against him, her words drowning inside his mouth. It was heaven. It was hell. And though Helen didn't want it to ever stop, she pushed him away.

"I told you to get out of here." Her voice was cold, flat, all signs of her fiery anger gone. "Go back to your party, your friends, your fiancée."

"My fiancée! I don't—" Marsh went silent, his eyes incredulous. "You're jealous?" The incredulity changed to wonder. "Helen, you're jealous."

Helen stepped back warily, unsure of his awed tone, the light that leaped into his eyes.

"Helen, love," Marsh murmured, "that girl is Grant's sister. She's been another Kris to me. That engagement party tonight was for her and a young guy named Robert, who decided he couldn't live another day without her. Just exactly as I decided the same about you in January." He walked to her slowly, drew her gently into his arms. "Nothing's changed that," he whispered. "Nothing ever will."

Tiny fingers crawled up Helen's scalp, and she experienced that eerie sensation he'd caused before.

"Oh, Marsh."

"What's-his-name has got to go," he groaned. "Helen, love, haven't you realized yet that we belong to each other, together? I won't let you send me away again. I can't and continue to function normally."

"What's-his-name is the husband of my best friend," Helen explained softly, her hand going to his face with the need to touch him. "She and I together successfully brought their first child into the world late this afternoon. He insisted on buying me dinner. That's what we were celebrating."

"Oh, God." His mouth moved over her face as if imprinting her likeness on his lips. "I don't ever want to live through a period like the last couple of hours again. Helen, I was so mad, I thought I'd blow apart. The thought of you with another man—" He shuddered and brought his mouth back to hers to kiss her violently.

"I know," she whispered when she could breathe again. "I was going through the same thing." Her voice went rough. "Marsh, where have you been these past weeks? I was sick with worry." Before he could answer, she slid her fingers over his lips, shook her head. "No, it doesn't matter. I love you. I want to spend the rest of my life with you. With commitments or without. With strings or without. That doesn't matter either." Then, very softly, she repeated his words of weeks ago. "The only thing that does matter is when you finally do come, from the office, or wherever, you'll be coming to me."

The sunshine, streaming through the bedroom windows, had a golden autumnal glow. Marsh, whistling softly, came through the bedroom door.

"Coffee's ready and the juice is poured, love. Are you going to laze away half the holiday in bed or are you going to get up and have breakfast with me?"

At the mention of food Helen groaned and rolled onto her side away from him.

A smile curving his lips, Marsh sauntered to Helen's

side of the bed, dropped onto his haunches, leaned forward, and tickled her ear with his tongue.

"If you're not up in thirty seconds, I'm going to crawl back in there with you, and I don't care if we never make it to Mother's for Thanksgiving dinner."

With a murmured "Good morning," Helen slid one arm around his neck and sought the lips now teasing her cheek. When his wake-up kiss started to deepen, she pushed gently against his shoulders. "Go back to the kitchen," Helen whispered breathlessly, evading his still-hungry mouth. "I'll be with you in a minute."

Marsh grinned, stole another quick kiss, then rose and strolled out of the room, again whistling softly.

After rinsing her face and brushing her teeth, Helen followed him to the kitchen, impatient with the weariness of her body. As she entered the kitchen the room swirled before her eyes, and groaning a soft protest against the light-headedness, she grasped the back of a kitchen chair.

"Helen?" Marsh's sharp tone barely penetrated the mistiness, but she felt his strength when he scooped her up into his arms. "What's the matter? Are you coming down with something?" The questions were rapped anxiously at her as he strode through the living room into the bedroom.

"No, Marsh, I'm not sick." Off her feet she felt the fuzziness pass and she smiled weakly at him. "I'm pregnant."

Marsh froze. Even his face looked frozen. "How?" At her arched glance he sighed, "I mean, I thought you were taking precautions."

"I stopped."

"Why, Helen? I told you it didn't matter."

"It suddenly mattered very much to me." She hid her face against his chest as he set her on her feet. "I wanted to have our baby, Marsh."

The sound of his sharply indrawn breath came clearly to her as he turned her around in his arms, then spread his hands wide over her still flat belly. "Is it safe for you, love?"

"Yes, Marsh. I'm seeing an excellent obstetrician."

"Are you sure?" he murmured against her hair. "Are you very, very sure?"

"Very, very sure." Helen's hands covered his, the narrow gold band on her left ring finger brushing against its counterpart on his. "It will be all right, I promise you. We are going to have a beautiful baby, Marsh."

Love—the way you want it!

Candlelight Romances

		TITLE NO.	
☐ A MAN OF HER CHOOSING by Nina Pykare	$1.50	#554	(15133-3)
☐ PASSING FANCY by Mary Linn Roby	$1.50	#555	(16770-1)
☐ THE DEMON COUNT by Anne Stuart	$1.25	#557	(11906-5)
☐ WHERE SHADOWS LINGER by Janis Susan May	$1.25	#556	(19777-5)
☐ OMEN FOR LOVE by Esther Boyd	$1.25	#552	(16108-8)
☐ MAYBE TOMORROW by Marie Pershing	$1.25	#553	(14909-6)
☐ LOVE IN DISGUISE by Nina Pykare	$1.50	#548	(15229-1)
☐ THE RUNAWAY HEIRESS by Lillian Cheatham	$1.50	#549	(18083-X)
☐ HOME TO THE HIGHLANDS by Jessica Eliot	$1.25	#550	(13104-9)
☐ DARK LEGACY by Candace Connell	$1.25	#551	(11771-2)
☐ LEGACY OF THE HEART by Lorena McCourtney	$1.25	#546	(15645-9)
☐ THE SLEEPING HEIRESS by Phyllis Taylor Pianka	$1.50	#543	(17551-8)
☐ DAISY by Jennie Tremaine	$1.50	#542	(11683-X)
☐ RING THE BELL SOFTLY by Margaret James	$1.25	#545	(17626-3)
☐ GUARDIAN OF INNOCENCE by Judy Boynton	$1.25	#544	(11862-X)
☐ THE LONG ENCHANTMENT by Helen Nuelle	$1.25	#540	(15407-3)
☐ SECRET LONGINGS by Nancy Kennedy	$1.25	#541	(17609-3)

At your local bookstore or use this handy coupon for ordering:

Dell **DELL BOOKS**
P.O. BOX 1000, PINEBROOK, N.J. 07058

Please send me the books I have checked above. I am enclosing $ _____
(please add 75¢ per copy to cover postage and handling). Send check or money order—no cash or C.O.D.'s. Please allow up to 8 weeks for shipment.

Mr/Mrs/Miss _____

Address _____

City _____ State/Zip _____

INTRODUCING...

The Romance Magazine For The 1980's

Each exciting issue contains a full-length romance novel — the kind of first-love story we all dream about...

PLUS

other wonderful features such as a travelogue to the world's most romantic spots, advice about your romantic problems, a quiz to find the ideal mate for you and much, much more.

ROMANTIQUE: A complete novel of romance, plus a whole world of romantic features.

ROMANTIQUE: Wherever magazines are sold. Or write Romantique Magazine, Dept. C-1, 41 East 42nd Street, New York, N.Y. 10017

INTERNATIONALLY DISTRIBUTED BY DELL DISTRIBUTING, INC.

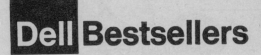

Dell Bestsellers

- ☐ SHOGUN by James Clavell $3.50 (17800-2)
- ☐ JUST ABOVE MY HEAD
  by James Baldwin $3.50 (14777-8)
- ☐ FIREBRAND'S WOMAN
  by Vanessa Royall $2.95 (12597-9)
- ☐ THE ESTABLISHMENT by Howard Fast $3.25 (12296-1)
- ☐ LOVING by Danielle Steel $2.75 (14684-4)
- ☐ THE TOP OF THE HILL by Irwin Shaw $2.95 (18976-4)
- ☐ JAILBIRD by Kurt Vonnegut $3.25 (15447-2)
- ☐ THE ENGLISH HEIRESS
  by Roberta Gellis $2.50 (12141-8)
- ☐ EFFIGIES by William K. Wells $2.95 (12245-7)
- ☐ FRENCHMAN'S MISTRESS
  by Irene Michaels $2.75 (12545-6)
- ☐ ALL WE KNOW OF HEAVEN
  by Dore Mullen $2.50 (10178-6)
- ☐ THE POWERS THAT BE
  by David Halberstam $3.50 (16997-6)
- ☐ THE LURE by Felice Picano $2.75 (15081-7)
- ☐ THE SETTLERS
  by William Stuart Long $2.95 (15923-7)
- ☐ CLASS REUNION by Rona Jaffe $2.75 (11408-X)
- ☐ TAI-PAN by James Clavell $3.25 (18462-2)
- ☐ KING RAT by James Clavell $2.50 (14546-5)
- ☐ RICH MAN, POOR MAN by Irwin Shaw $2.95 (17424-4)
- ☐ THE IMMIGRANTS by Howard Fast $3.25 (14175-3)
- ☐ TO LOVE AGAIN by Danielle Steel $2.50 (18631-5)

At your local bookstore or use this handy coupon for ordering:

**DELL BOOKS
P.O. BOX 1000, PINEBROOK, N.J. 07058**

Please send me the books I have checked above. I am enclosing $_____
(please add 75¢ per copy to cover postage and handling). Send check or money order—no cash or C.O.D.'s. Please allow up to 8 weeks for shipment.

Mr/Mrs/Miss _____

Address _____

City _____ State/Zip _____